The Lights of Heaven

Séamus Ó Grianna

The Lights of Heaven

stories and essays

selected and edited by
Nollaig Mac Congáil

ARLEN
HOUSE

First published by Arlen House in 2006

Arlen House
PO Box 222
Galway
Ireland
arlenhouse@gmail.com
Phone/Fax 086 8207617

ISBN   1-903631-37-8, paperback

Cover photo courtesy of Tarlach McGonagle
Typesetting: Arlen House
Printed by: Colourbooks, Dublin

CONTENTS

Acknowledgements

I would like to thank Séamus Ó Grianna's son Feilimí for allowing me to reproduce these stories here and for generously donating the manuscripts to the James Hardiman Library, National University of Ireland, Galway.

Tá mé buíoch d'fhoireann Leabharlann James Hardiman, OÉ, Gaillimh, as a gcabhair agus as a gcuidiú agus mé i mbun an taighde seo, agus don Ollscoil féin as tacaíocht a thabhairt don saothar seo.

Tá buíochas tuillte fosta ag beirt scoláirí ar spéis leo an réimse léinn seo, mar atá, An tOllamh Philip O'Leary agus an Dr. Lillis Ó Laoire.

Caithfidh mé buíochas a ghabháil le Ríona as a cuidiú le réiteach an ábhair seo, le Tarlach as grianghraf a sholáthar agus mo ghríosú i gceann na hoibre seo, agus le Conall as a acmhainn grinn.

Buíochas fosta leis an Dr. A.J. Moriarty as a eolas fairsing faoi chuile rud a rann liom.

FOREWORD

This book is a sequel to the unique collection of stories *The Sea's Revenge and Other Stories* (Mercier Press, 2003) and includes the last of the stories translated by Séamus Ó Grianna as well as some original stories by him which he penned near the end of his life. Following in the vein of the first collection, these stories depict the Donegal *Gaeltacht* life of yesteryear: life on the seaboard and the dangers and superstitions pertaining to it; feats of prowess at home and abroad, on land and sea; love sought, love gained, love lost, love better lost; politics and poetry. This vanished world is lovingly and sometimes bitterly depicted by the author who spent most of his creative life reconstructing his version of that world according to his own taste, insight and emphasis. His later, original stories in English reflect his disillusion with the aftermath of the fight for independence.

The essays in this collection span different decades of Séamus Ó Grianna's life and reflect his views on Gaelic literature, and the Government's and the Language Movement's policies regarding the Irish Language. Some of these essays relate to his active support for the controversial Language Freedom Movement in the 1960s.

THE RIVALS[1]

The two girls were born and brought up in the townland of Rosmore, by the sea. One of them was called Dolly. The other's name was Shewan. They were about the same age. As small children they played together on the strand. They went to school together. One would think they were bosom pals. Yet, deep down in their hearts, they disliked each other.

Each of them had an advantage over the other. Shewan's people kept a small grocery shop, which meant that they were better off than their neighbours. Dolly's people were very poor. Shewan was not by any means good-looking. She was long and thin and shapeless. Her shoulders were narrow and her chest was flat. Dolly was a beauty. She had all the attributes that our poets have sung about down the ages. Her eyes were like stars, her teeth like pearls, her clusters of brown curls down her neck and shoulders. There was magic in the sound of her voice; and her burst of rippling laughter would gladden the heart of the most cynical man that ever lived.

When the girls were about twelve years of age her mother bought Shewan a nice dress, with shoes to match. Poor Dolly was in rags and in her bare feet. She cried her eyes out for a whole day. This was Shewan's round. And Dolly will neither forgive nor forget: 'There are wrongs to wash away, there are memories to destroy'.

The years passed and the two girls grew to womanhood. To all appearances they were great friends. Their attitude towards each other seemed charming. But they were as ready to sting as they were to charm, when the occasion arose. They were rivals all the time. Which of them would be the first to get married? That would be a decisive victory. Each of them had their strong points in the matrimonial market. Shewan was expected to get a handsome dowry, Dolly would have none. Shewan was plain and unattractive, Dolly was the star of the Rosses.

II

Donal O'Boyle was by far the finest young man in the parish, but from the point of view of marriage, he had nothing else to recommend him. At the age of eighteen he went across to Scotland to work and came under the influence of some of the toughest navvies of the day – men like Joe Wurraghy, Ginger Diffy and Black Jimmy Boyle. After seven years Donal came back home as poor as he was the day he left it. He had drunk and gambled every penny he had earned.

Many a young girl looked at him with longing eyes and said to herself she would like to have him for a husband, if only she could be sure that he would mend his ways. But would it be possible to tame him? Would marriage make him give up the drink and the fighting? His mother was anxious to see him 'taken off the roads of Scotland', as she put it. But who would have him? Shewan? Of course she was not by any means a match for him as far as looks went. But other things had to be reckoned with. Shewan would have a bit of money. They could buy a little holding for themselves … Shewan was consulted by Donal's mother. She was prepared to take the risk. And we will leave her for a while to try her luck.

Away up at the foot of the hills, in a place called the Dark Glen, lived Long Lanty. He was forty years of age when he decided to marry. Evidently it never occurred to him until his mother died.

He lived in a long, thatched house near the upper end of the glen. He had plenty of good grazing moorland, and always kept a good stock of cattle and sheep. He was a handy man about a house. He could wash his clothes and darn his socks and look after the fowl. He had had plenty of practice in these domestic duties, for the old woman had been crippled with rheumatism for years before she died. In addition to the qualifications we have mentioned, Lanty could knit. This was indeed a rare accomplishment. For it is not recorded in the history of the Rosses that any other man ever took a set of knitting needles in his hands.

But when it came to looking for a wife Lanty had his drawbacks. He was not the type that would make a romantic appeal to a girl. He never wore anything but undyed, homespun trousers and a sleeved waistcoat of the same material. His long, straight hair came down over his neck, as if he wore it to keep himself warm. He spoke in a thin piping voice that gave the impression that he was very old, although he was only about forty years.

He wanted a wife. Where would he look for one? He might never have dreamt of coming down as far as Rosmore if it had not been suggested to him. A woman from the 'lower country' was married in the townland next to the Dark Glen. It was she suggested Shewan to Lanty. 'A good girl', said she. 'And splendid worker and a first-class housekeeper. And she'll have a nice penny to get. The money is yonder. I know it … If you like I'll go down and ask her for you'.

Shewan's father and mother were delighted with the proposal. As for Shewan herself she was willing enough, but she was playing for time. She had often met Donal O'Boyle since he had come home from Scotland. He was polite and friendly in her company. And hadn't her mother let it be known that she was anxious to make the match? On the whole the circumstances were such as to plant a tiny seed of hope in Shewan's breast. That was why she did not accept Long Lanty's offer straight away. But she did not refuse it either. It had been sprung on her suddenly, she said. She wanted time to make up her mind. And Long Lanty was willing to await the outcome of her deliberations.

Soon afterwards it began to be whispered in Rosmore that Donal O'Boyle was going to marry Shewan. The young man's mother was known to be pushing the negotiations for all she was worth. And Donal himself, with his bitter experience of an Irish navvy's life in Scotland, was supposed to be coming round to the view that a little home in the Rosses was better than the hut and the model and the tramp from Kinlochlevin to Rosythe. The rumour could become a certainty any day. All the signs pointed to it.

It was then that Dolly stepped into the ring. 'This round is going to be mine', she said to herself. 'A vital round it is too'.

She tossed her nut-brown curls to the sky. She laughed her burst of joyous musical laughter. In a word she turned the battery of charms on Donal O'Boyle. He surrendered without a struggle … It was midsummer at the time. They decided to get married on the fourth of August following – Lammas Fair Day in the Rosses.

Shewan sent word to Long Lanty that she was accepting him and that she wanted to get married on the fourth of August.

Dolly and Shewan met on a Sunday afternoon and they strolled down to the cliffs at the seashore. They had to congratulate one another and renew their pledges of everlasting friendship.

'Just imagine', said Shewan. 'The two of us getting married the same day. In a way it makes me sad to think that this is our last summer together'.

'And me, too', said Dolly. 'Sometimes I ask myself if we would not be happier if we never got married but just live our lives here beside one another'.

'I sometimes think the same', said Shewan. 'But then again we won't be always young. I suppose after all it is natural to get married. It seems the right thing to do. But we must not let marriage put an end to our companionship. We must visit one another as often as possible'.

'Of course we will', agreed Dolly.

'You are getting a fine man, Dolly', said Shewan, after a pause. 'The finest man in the three parishes. In the past he was a bit wild and fond of the drink. But I am sure he will settle down. Lots of men do. Look at Johnny Andy over there in Rinnamona and the way he gave up the drink and settled down when he got married. Donal will do the same thing; wait till you see. Everything will be all right. We'll pray for him'.

'I don't know anything about the man you are getting married to', said Dolly, 'but, by all accounts, he is a good man. A good, sensible man with land and stock and money. And, mind you, that is something in these hard times. He is a bit older than you, they say. But that does not matter much. The difference is on the right side. A woman gets older much sooner than a man'.

And each of them said in her own mind:

Dolly: 'Well, I would not marry that old, withered, lifeless *soogan* if there wasn't another man left on the ridge of the world. Perhaps she imagines that she'll improve him, but she will have her work cut out for herself. She'll have to go at him with a shears and cut his hair. Then she will have to scrub his neck and to trim his fingernails. I wonder will he get married in the homespun-sleeved waistcoat?'

Shewan: 'She was always poor. Born in poverty and reared in poverty. But it is only beginning. Wait till she is a few years married to that drunken wastrel. Then she'll know. She has nothing but contempt for the man I am marrying. I know it. I see the badness in her eyes. But the day will come when I will lower her pride. I will visit her some fine Sunday, dressed in my best. I'll walk in on her. She will be sitting in her rags over a dying fire with her bare toes in the ashes'.

III

For a year or two after he got married, Donal O'Boyle settled down. But then his old habits got the better of him again. He used to go to Scotland to work for the summer season but, very often, he spent the most of what he earned. And, of course, his wife and children suffered as a result. They were in constant poverty. Sometimes they were hungry. Dolly had not a shoe to her foot. On Sundays she would hide herself in the lower corner of the church, just inside the door, and come out at the Last Gospel. Then she would run home across the bog road as fast as she could – looking behind her like a hunted animal for fear anyone was overtaking her.

Poor Dolly. She had a hard life of it. And still she loved her man with an abiding, changeless love. She knew he was not indifferent to her woes. He made several promises to mend his ways. He made several honest attempts but he always relapsed.

At last he made one desperate resolve to give up his bad habits one for all. There was only one way of doing it. Not alone must he resolve never again to taste drink under any circumstances, but he must keep away from the company of every man who might lead him astray. He was ostracising himself from his friends and relations and neighbours for the rest of his life. It was hard, very hard. But desperate diseases needed desperate remedies. It was on the eve of Patrick's Day that he made this resolution. And he meant to keep it. But he would inaugurate the new regime in a way that would make a lasting impression on him. He would take one last, fond look at the light that had dazzled him for years; he would follow the bands to Dungloe on the morrow. It would be his last outing. The following year, and every year while he lived, he would come straight home from Mass on Patrick's Day. Just a farewell march, it was all he asked for.

Dolly thought his request was reasonable. But Donal had no money. Dolly's heart softened again. She had a few shillings saved – the beginning of a fund to buy herself a pair of shoes – and she gave it to him.

As if it were Donal's firm intention to make this Patrick's Day march his last outing, it was always his firm intention not to get drunk. He would drown the shamrock. He would listen to the music of the bands and enjoy it. In the evening he would come and say good-bye forever to the joys and to the follies of youth.

He followed the bands to Dungloe. There he met two neighbours. They went into a pub. Donal bought a round of drinks. In due course one of the men wanted to buy a second round. Donal would not consent. 'Decidedly not', said he. 'I'll wait for at least two hours. I have firmly made up my mind not to get drunk today – my last Patrick's Day out. I see a gang of Carnamaddy men down there on the bridge. I beat three of them in Broxburn one night last year. They will be after me today. But I can dodge them. That is why I want to keep sober, today above all days'.

Later on one of the Carnamaddy men accosted Donal and challenged him to fight. Donal refused to accept the challenge. 'No, you won't fight today', said the other man. 'But you would if you had a gang of your townies around you, armed with knuckle-duster and loaded batons, like you had in Broxburn last year'.

This was too much for a clean fighter who, even in self-defence against unfair odds, had never used any weapon except his fists. He hit the Carnamaddy man and knocked him down. Three more made a rush at him. Donal piled them on top of one another. A big policeman came running to the scene of the conflict with his baton drawn. He aimed a blow at Donal. Donal side-stepped. Then he hit the policeman and knocked him clean over the wall of the bridge. Reinforcements rushed to the spot. Donal knocked down a second and third policeman. At last he was overpowered by sheer weight of numbers and brought to the barracks. The following day he was taken to Derry jail under a heavy escort.

IV

Donal O'Boyle was in Derry jail awaiting his trial. Knowledgeable men were weighing the charges against him and anticipated the sentence. Beat four Carnamaddy men. Well, that was not very serious. But beat three policemen, and one of them badly, in discharge of their lawful duty, that was a grave offence indeed … Five years' penal servitude, at the very least!

Shewan, of course, heard the news, and welcome news it was to her. This would be *her* round, she concluded. She would go down to Rosmore and offer Dolly her sympathy. Then she would come to her aid. She would suggest a public subscription. She decided to head the list herself with three pounds. Dolly would have no alternative but to accept this humiliating offer.

Some days afterwards Shewan decided to set out on her mission. 'I am going down to Rosmore', she said to Long Lanty. 'I want to see Dolly, the wife of that rascal who is in Derry jail for beating policemen in Dungloe on Patrick's Day'.

'Had he any sense?' said Lanty. 'Beating policemen! Sure he'll be transported to Van Diemen's Land for that awful crime'.

'And he deserves it', said Shewan. 'I have no pity for him. I haven't much for Dolly for that matter. She is as bad as himself. She has no sense of shame. Never had. Nor any of her breed. But I pity the poor, innocent children. Something must be done to save them from dying of hunger'.

On the afternoon of that day Shewan arrived in Rosmore dressed in her best – from her buttoned boots to her black cashmere shawl. As she crossed the threshold of the poor, little cabin Dolly advanced to meet her with outstretched arms. '*Masha*, Shewan, *achree*, and how are you at all at all. Sure it's right glad I am to see you. And how is the good man himself? Sit here. On this chair beside me. He have lots of things to say to each other. It's so long since we met. Lots of things about the old days. Just yesterday I was thinking of our childhood days'.

'I am sorry for your trouble, Dolly', said Shewan rather nervously. 'Very sorry indeed … Poor Donal, it was too bad what happened him'.

'It could not have been otherwise in the end', said Dolly. 'What can one man do against a dozen? And it took a dozen of them to put him down and put the handcuffs on him. But he put up a dandy fight. He was knocking them down like ninepins. They say it was the greatest fight he ever fought', she concluded proudly, like a member of Napoleon's Old Guard describing Marshal Ney's last desperate dash at Waterloo.

'Yes, Dolly', pursued Shewan, ignoring the dandy fight. 'I would have come down sooner but we were very busy. Between cows and sheep and fowl, and preparing for the spring work, it is so hard to get away. But this morning I said to myself there are other things in life besides making money. 'Whatever about the work', says I to myself, 'I must go down to poor Dolly and see what can be done for her'. For this is a cruel blow. A very cruel blow. You must be sad and lonely. But, as the old people used to say, God never shut one door without opening another. We must see to it that the innocent won't suffer'.

'Sad and lonely', said Dolly, preparing for the attack. 'Well, whatever about the sadness at times, I am not lonely. Haven't I my children? How could I ever be lonely with my little birdies round me in the nest? Sure I couldn't', she continued, as she took up her youngest child and held it high over her head. She tickled its ribs with her fingers and began talking to it in baby language. 'Sure I'm not lonely. How could your mammy ma be lonely when she has her own toodlums woodlums?'

'It is a pity that poor Donal didn't stay at home on Patrick's Day', ventured Shewan.

'He never did', replied Dolly. 'Sure he didn't?' said she, addressing herself again to the child. 'Sure your own dadsy-wadsy never stayed at home on Patrick's Day? Your own dadsy-wadsy is a man ... I must put turf on the fire and boil the kettle till we have a sup of tea and a chat as we used to have in the old days. I can't tell you, Shewan, how glad I am to see you after all the years. Why don't you come down oftener? I would go to the Dark Glen to see you only I cannot get away'.

On her way out for the turf she began playing with the other children. She took one of them up and swung it round three times. The children were delighted that their mammy had shaken off her sadness and her sorrow and was again laughing and playing with them.

Shewan felt herself being defeated. She was up against a force she had not reckoned with. But she must say something.

'Dolly', she began, 'it would be a good thing for you if Donal O'Boyle were like the man I have'.

'What makes you think that?' asked Dolly.

'What I mean is this', replied Shewan, 'if he were like my man, he wouldn't be fighting and he'd never get into trouble. He would come straight home after Mass on Patrick's Day and leave others to follow the bands. And you would be a happy woman ... But what is done can't be undone. I am going to see to it that your children don't go hungry'.

Dolly's eyes blazed like two live coals. 'A good thing for me if Donal O'Boyle were like your man!' she said. 'As God is my judge, I prefer to have him the way he is. Five years they say he'll get for hitting three policemen and half-killing one of them. But if he were to get twenty years, if he were in Derry jail awaiting the hangman, I'd rather that than be married to a *cábánach* like what you have. Sure he is not a man at all. My poor, dear Shewan, I have all the pity in the world for you, so I have'.

Shewan got up and left without another word.

V

She set out on her journey homewards with a heavy step and a sore heart. O, God in heaven, the bitter, burning, cruel things that Dolly had said to her!

It was coming on to nightfall when she arrived home. She stood for a moment and looked up the Dark Glen. It was darker than ever it had been before. Dark and lonely and lifeless. She looked at the long, rambling, thatched house that was her home. Four walls and a roof that kept the wind and rain from her. That was all.

Long Lanty came out of the henhouse with a tin basin in his hand. He had to stoop down to get through the low doorway.

'Back again?' he said lightly.

'Back again', said Shewan in a tired voice.

'The speckled hen is laying again', said Lanty. 'She'll continue laying from now on till next Christmas. And look at the size of him!' said he, holding up an egg between his finger and thumb.

'Leave them inside on the dresser', said Shewan without looking at the eggs.

They went into the house together. Lanty put the basin of eggs down on the ledge of the dresser. Shewan took off her shawl and put it away. Then she sat on a low stool in the corner beside the fire. Lanty sat on another stool in the opposite corner and began to talk.

'Are you hungry?' he asked.

'No, I'm not', replied Shewan.

'The brown hen is going a-clocking', said Lanty. 'We must put a clutch under her. There's a woman has a very good breed of hens – Sally Vickey Andy in Drumard. I met her today when I was going out to the Black Gap to have a look at the lambs. She tells me they're great layers. From the Lagan she got them herself, about three years ago. She can let us have a dozen hatching eggs any time we want them'.

'Hm, hm'.

'Is there anything the matter with you?' asked Lanty.

'No, nothing'.

Lanty reached for his knitting. 'I did a good bit last night', said he, holding up the stocking. 'I'll have it as far as the narrows tomorrow night if God spares me. Great yarn that of Mickey Kennedy's. Try a round of it till you see how smooth it runs', said he, reaching the stocking to Shewan.

She made no move to take it from him. She sat there with her hands clasped in her lap.

'What is wrong with you?' he asked rather anxiously.

She looked across at him.

'For God Almighty's sake', said she. 'Put away the knitting and give over your old woman's talk and habits. Stop talking about hens and eggs and clutches. Try to be a man. At least try. Tomorrow is the fair day in Benmore. Go down to the fair and get drunk. Kick something, if it were only a goat's kid in the cattle market. Knock down something and break it if it were only a soap-box with an apple-woman's tray on it'.

Long Lanty, amazed and dumbfounded, got up and left the knitting on the window-sill. Then he came back on his stool in the corner with his face turned away from his wife and down towards the lower end of the long kitchen.

And so they sat, each of them staring blankly into space ... The fire burned low and the shadows ceased to dance on the walls. The darkness thickened inside the house. Neither Lanty nor Shewan made a move to light the lamp. They just sat there in the silent darkness like two ghosts.

A person passing by the doorstep outside would think there was nothing with life in it in the house except that was chirping a cranny beside the fireplace.

Note

1   This is an English version of the story 'Cora an tSaoghail' which is published in *An Clár is an Fhoireann* (An Gúm, 1955), 7-13.

THE BEGGAR'S FUNERAL[1]

Father O'Reilly was getting old and tired. One winter's night he was sitting alone by his fireside, musing to himself and listening to the moan of the wind in the chimney and to the hiss of the driven snow against the window.

The priest was thinking over his past life. He was thinking of the aims and ambitions and grand schemes he had when he was young, of the much he had planned and the little he had accomplished.

One of his aims in life from the day of his ordination was to stamp out drunkenness in every parish he should be sent to minister in. Drunkenness, he maintained, was at the root of all evil. Often in his sermons he thundered against it with all the force of eloquence, with all the sincerity that came of a settled conviction.

'It is', he would say, 'a wicked thing for a human being to deprive himself of the reason that God gave him to put him above the level of the rest of the animal creation ... We often hear men talking about the freedom of our country. A noble thought. But what good would all the freedom in the world be to a nation of drunkards? ... We often heard it said that there is no harm in taking a drink. But the first drink nearly always calls for the second. The second calls for the third. After that you are gone down the slippery slope with nothing to catch hold of. There is only one way to avoid getting drunk and that is by not tasting it at all. At all, I say. Under no circumstances, if you want to save yourselves from ruin, in this world and in the next'.

The young lads in the village – those hardly out of their teens – were a particular source of worry to him. He was afraid of the influence that one Larry Maguire might have over them. Larry was a fine man, about twenty-five years of age. Nobody ever saw him drunk but he could take a glass or two at any time and he was fond of jolly company. 'His is just the kind of man that youngsters would like to imitate', the priest would say to himself. 'And, to crown it all, he has the voice of an angel. I listened to him a few times myself without letting him see me. Maybe I should have said: 'God forgive me' for having listened on one occasion'.

This particular night Father O'Reilly was looking into the fire, as if he saw pictures of the past in the glowing coals. He saw one picture that made him sad. It was the picture of a young man of tall, slight build, with a bronze complexion and raven, black hair. His name was Cathal McElgunn or Cathal Buí[2] as he had been called at home.

James O'Reilly and Cathal Buí were class-mates in the college in Salamanca. They were great friends. They were from the same diocese and O'Reilly hoped that when they returned to Ireland as priests they would be at least within visiting distance of each other. They would keep up their friendship all their lifetime! But, in the course of time, Cathal Buí began to change. He became silent. Sometimes he looked like a man who was fighting a battle with himself. He was between two minds. The world, with its attractions for youth, was beckoning him. Sometimes he would dismiss the thought as the prompting of the Devil, against which all mortals must fight and pray. But then the maddening thought would come to him that perhaps he had no vocation for the priesthood. And, if he hadn't, would he not be fulfilling God's will better as a layman? By marrying Molly Brady?

At last he decided. He told his companion he was leaving, without mentioning Molly Brady's name. O'Reilly tried to persuade him to remain. 'This is only a test of your faith', he pleaded. 'Patience and prayers will bring you through it'.

But it was no use. Cathal Buí left the college one fine summer's morning and went out into the world. After a time he took to drinking. The last that father O'Reilly heard of him was that he was a wandering pedlar somewhere in the region beyond Loch Macnean, and that he had composed songs that were very popular not alone in his native district but in places as far away as Donegal.

Father O'Reilly recalled the first time he had heard Cathal Buí's most famous song – 'The Yellow Bittern'.[3] It was one fair day he went to the village to see that the men did not linger long in the public houses. 'Especially that rascal Larry Maguire. They would remain there for hours listening to him singing'. When Father O'Reilly came opposite the door of the public house he heard someone singing. It was the rascal Larry Maguire singing 'The Yellow Bittern'. The priest went round behind a cart, where he would not be seen, and he stood there listening until the singer had finished.

I remember one verse of it, thought the priest to himself the night he sat musing by the fireside.

> My darling told me to drink no more,
> For my life would be o'er in a very short while,
> I told her 'twas drink gave me health and strength
> And lengthen'd the road for many a mile.
> Oh! Saw you the bird of the long smooth neck,
> How he got his death from the drouth at last?
> Come, son of my soul, and drain your cup,
> For you'll get no sup when your life is past.

It is pure paganism, said Father O'Reilly in his own mind. An absolutely pagan conception of life and death … But, by heaven, he could sing, pagan and all as he was … I wonder if he is still alive? He hardly is. I should think that he is dead long ago, and that his own prophecy was fulfilled – that there wasn't a tear shed over his grave the day he was buried!

II

The wind was rising and driving the snow against the window with still greater force. It was a night that would move a man to study, or to dream. But Father O'Reilly was in no mood for reading. The thoughts that had come into his head left him strangely sad. He sat there looking at the dying embers of the fire. At last he dozed off to sleep.

He was dreaming. He was in Spain. It was early summer. The sky overhead was clear and blue. He saw the palm trees on the sidewalks of the street. He saw men and women sitting under their shade – men and women who, to all appearances, were supremely happy … In the course of time his companion and he will be ordained and they will go back to Ireland together. But why this change in the companion? Why the long periods of silence? Why does he look sadly and longingly over the walls at times …?

There was a loud knock at the door. It was repeated a second time. Father O'Reilly awoke with a start. He got up and went to the door and opened it. There was a man outside on the doorstep. He was covered with snow from head to foot. 'Come in', said the priest, holding the door open. The man stepped inside. He was trying to keep as far from the priest as possible.

'Someone wants me?' asked Father O'Reilly.

'Yes, Father, and as soon as you can go'.

'So it's you, Larry Maguire. Well, who wants me?'

'I don't know who it is, Father'.

'You don't know? You have been drinking. I can smell it off you'.

'I took only one wee glass, Father, just one wee sup to keep the cold from freezing the marrow of my bones this cruel night'.

'You have come for the priest and you can't remember who wants him. It took more than one wee glass to put you in that state'.

'I beg your pardon, Father. I meant to say I did not know the name of the sick person. Nobody does. But I know where he is. Out in the Windy Gap'.

'The Windy Gap? Sure there hasn't been a soul living there for years. There is no house in the Gap, only an old shack that people put sheep in at times'.

'And that is where the sick man is lying'.

'You don't know his name?'

'I don't, Father. Nobody does, as I've said. It is an old beggar man. He came to the Gap last week and went to the old hut. The neighbours saw him coming. They brought him some food and straw and old sacks to make a bed. It was thought he would leave the next day. But that night it began to snow and it is snowing since. Now he believes he is dying and he wants the priest'.

'Very good, Larry', said Father O'Reilly, getting ready. 'You have done your duty. Now I must do mine … You know the short-cut to the Gap? Good. Give me your hand … I hope I get there in time'.

The wind was driving the snow against their faces. But

they plodded along determinedly. At last they came to the hut where the old beggar man lay dying.

The priest went inside. He found three men sitting round a fire they had made with fir rootlets. A candle stuck in a bottle cast a dim yellow light on everything in the hut. In the corner there was a heap of straw and a few old sacks. The priest took the candle and went to the 'bedside'. There he found a gaunt, withered, old man with hair as white as the snow that was falling outside.

'Thank God I was in time', said the priest. The men went out and round to the lee side of the hut. Larry Maguire was there already. It was a cruel night. A night that Death would be abroad.

The men outside were shivering with cold. 'I am drenched to the skin and frozen over it', said Larry Maguire. 'I feel the cold going through the marrow of my bones'.

'If you had a few good glasses of punch', said one of the others, 'you would soon forget all about the cold in the marrow of your bones'.

'If I had all the punch that was ever brewed', said Larry, 'I would not touch a drop of it – at least not until I'd be back after leaving Father O'Reilly at home. I only took a wee drop before I went down for him and didn't he smell it off me as soon as I put my head inside the door. Only he was in too big a hurry I'd have got a lecture from him that I would remember'.

'He seems to have his knife in you, Larry', said one of the men.

'Sometimes I think he has', said Larry, 'other times I think he likes me. As if he were between two minds whether he should bless me or curse me. One day last year – it was the day after the fair – I met him. His eyes lit up with gladness. He spoke to me in a very friendly tone. Then, all of a sudden, his face darkened, as if he had remembered that I was a child of the Devil. 'I heard you were singing in Meegan's pub yesterday', he said, and he gave me a look that frightened me. The truth of the story is that he was hiding behind a cart listening to my song'.

'Isn't it a strange thing', said one of the others. 'If it were allowed for me I would say that it is in getting drunk the harm is, not in taking a drink when a man needs one, or when he is enjoying himself. But, according to him, no one should taste it at all, at all'.

'They say', said a third man, 'that it was a shock he got long ago when he was in the college in Spain. There was a young man there along with him – a man from away beyond the hills. He refused to become a priest and he left the college. He came back to Ireland. Later on, he took to drink. Ever since, Father O'Reilly hates the mention of the word drink. And sure he is wrong there – with all due respect to his cloth. Why shouldn't we have a drink tonight to keep the wicked cold out of our bones? As well forbid us to warm ourselves at the fire because someone got burned once upon a time'.

The priest came out. He was choking with emotion when he spoke. 'We must take the poor man out of this wretched hut if he lives till morning', said he. 'I am sitting up with him. One of you can sit along with me. The rest of you can go home … No, not you, Larry Maguire. Go home. You must be drenched to the skin'.

Three of the men left for home. The fourth went into the hut along with the priest.

The old beggar was lying on the straw in the corner. There was a calm, peaceful expression on his face. At times he opened and closed the fingers of one hand, as if trying to clutch at something. But most of the time he lay there with his eyes closed as if he were fast asleep. The priest had a roll of manuscripts in his hand which he tried to read out at times by the light of the candle.

The night passed. Shortly before dawn it was noticed that the dying man became restless. The priest hurriedly stuffed the manuscript into the pocket of his overcoat. He knelt beside the pallet and began to recite the Prayers for the Dying ... A gurgling sound came from the old man's throat. It was the end. He passed away as the first streaks of dawn struggled through the snow-laden skies.

'May God rest his soul', said the priest, putting his hand to his eyes as if he were wiping away a tear.

III

'We must make arrangements to have him buried tomorrow', said the priest later on to some of the men from the neighbourhood. 'I have ordered the coffin. We must start early. There's a good nine miles from here to Cashel'.

'To Cashel!' replied one of the men in surprise. 'Begging your pardon, Father, but why should we have to carry him all the way to Cashel in this weather? Can't we bury him in Kilmore? After all, he is a stranger from the Lord knows where. It is not the same as if his people were buried in Cashel'.

'We must bring him to Cashel', persisted the priest. 'It is his own wish. Seems he believed in a tradition that the body of a saint is buried at Cashel and that all who are buried in that graveyard will be with the saint at the Resurrection'.

'Do you believe in that story, Father, if it's no harm to ask you?'

'Whether I believe in it or not is beside the point. The poor fellow expressed a wish to be buried in Cashel. He wrote it down on paper. I will read it for you all later on when I have time'.

It would be a long and weary journey, with the snow over two feet deep in the hollows. But the burial at Cashel would have one advantage: the journey was too long and the weather too severe for Father O'Reilly to go. And there was no necessity for him to go. The old graveyard was outside the boundaries of his parish. The priest at Cashel would officiate. Father O'Reilly would not go, could not go. That would leave the men free to take a few drinks that would lighten their hearts and keep the piercing cold out of the marrow of their bones!

But the men were wrong in supposing that Father O'Reilly would not accompany the beggar's remains to Cashel. He was at the hut in the Windy Gap when they lifted the coffin on their shoulders and set out. It was thought that he would turn back after a mile or two of the way had been travelled. But the priest walked on behind the coffin-bearers, mile after mile, until at last it became evident that he was going all the way to the old churchyard.

It had stopped snowing that morning but it began again around midday. The cortege plodded along, four men in their turn carrying the coffin. At last a long thatched house came into view. It was Owen O'Hanlon's pub in Ballintemple.

What a misfortune, thought the men, that the priest was along with them. How gladly they would, if they were allowed, go in and have a few drinks and rest their weary limbs. How badly they needed it after trudging through the snow since early morning carrying a coffin. All they could get now would be only, as the poet said, a fleeting glimpse of the glasses as they passed by the windows. But what was the use in sighing and wishing for the impossible!

'Leave down the coffin for a little while', said Father O'Reilly when they had come as far as the public house. 'Put it there on that low stone wall opposite the door … Now let you all go inside for a minute. Every one of you'.

The priest ordered a round of drinks. The men could not get over their surprise. They could scarcely believe their ears, or their eyes as they stood there looking at the row of glasses on the counter, as if they were afraid it was only a dream.

'Come on, men', said Father O'Reilly taking up his glass. 'Drink your drinks. This is only the first. You must have another at least. One solitary drink would hardly fulfil the dead man's wishes. And we must fulfil them to the letter. But, before you begin your second drink, I will call on Larry Maguire to sing 'The Yellow Bittern''.

'But excuse me, Father', protested Larry.

'Pardon me, Larry', replied the priest, 'but I will not excuse you. You have a fine voice and you can put life and feeling into 'The Yellow Bittern' if any man can. How I happen to know, that is another matter. Some day I may tell you … Stand there inside the door, so that you can see the coffin with the white snow on the lid of it. Now'.

'Very well done, Larry', said the priest. There is not another man in Ireland can sing that song like you … Now you will all have your second drink. It was the dead man's wish to be buried like this. He wrote it, shortly before he died. Here it is'.

> When death takes my spirit – and I feel that
> I'll soon get the call –
> You will lay me in Cashel beside yonder

Ivy-clad wall;
Going through Ballintemple you will sing one
Last lyric of mine,
And drink to my memory in goblets of flowing
Red wine.

They were beginning to warm up over the second drink when all of a sudden they heard a piercing wail coming from the far side of the road. They rushed to the door and windows. They were amazed at what they saw – an old woman bent over the coffin and keening in heart-rending tones.

The publican's wife went out and spoke to her. 'Will you come inside for a while, my poor woman, and warm yourself at the fire. You must be frozen from the cold, and perhaps you are hungry'.

'Thanks, Mrs. O'Hanlon', said the old woman. 'You were always kind. But I am not hungry. I will go inside in a minute, into the bar where the funeral party are. I have a duty to perform. A dead man's wish to fulfil'.

Shortly afterwards she came into the bar. She was a gaunt, withered, old woman, with her grey hair plastered to her cheeks from the wet. She wore a pair of men's hob-nailed boots, an old threadbare shawl and a dress that was nothing but shreds and patches.

The priest made room for her on the seat beside him and got Owen O'Hanlon to bring her a glass of hot punch.

She looked round at the men and saw that their glasses were nearly empty.

'Have another drink, men', she said. 'This one is on me'.

'Pardon me', said the priest. 'If the men feel like having another drink I'll pay for it. If I haven't the price of it I can easily get it'.

'Father', pleaded the old woman, 'would you deprive me the one and only little bit of happiness I can have on this blackest of black days?'

This was not the language of an ordinary beggar woman. It was a heart-rending appeal. There was some terrible tragedy behind it. The priest could not resist. 'Very good, my child', he said. 'Go ahead'.

The old woman took a small bundle from her bosom and handed it to the publican. It was a small handkerchief knotted together at the corners so as to form a pouch. 'Take what is yours out of that', she said. 'And please take all the coppers. It took me quite a time to collect it', she continued, addressing herself to the priest. 'Very humiliating going from door to door begging pennies. I could not do it for myself. I would rather lie down and die of hunger. I could do it only for the man I loved. For years I have been doing it. And when I would have a few shillings collected I would send it to him. A few weeks ago I heard he was in this part of the country and that he was ill. A few days ago word was brought to me that he was at a place called the Windy Gap. I took all my worldly store and set out to visit him. But you know how the weather turned out, Father. I only got there today. And when I was within a mile or so of the Gap I met the funeral. Oh! If I could have seen him before he died, even though he could not recognise me. If I could have seen even his dead face before they nailed down the coffin lid'.

Here she broke down and sobbed bitterly

'You knew him well?' asked the priest when the old woman had calmed down.

'Knew him, Father?' she said. 'I am the only one in the world who did know him. I knew his great heart and his great soul. I knew his weakness. I realised the agony he suffered trying to overcome it. I knew he felt he was condemned to misery in this world. But I also knew that he had an abiding hope of happiness in the next'.

'Had you known him for long?' asked the priest.

'Since he and I were young. But I had better tell the whole story, Father, if I am not boring you'.

'Not at all, my good woman. On the contrary, the slightest detail about his life interests me'.

'Well', resumed the old woman, 'the beginning of the story is about myself. I was an only child. My parents were well off. Comparatively speaking. My mother had great ambitions for me. She got the local hedge schoolmaster to teach me to read and write – Irish as well as English. Later on she got the priest to teach me some Latin. Finally she sent me to a convent school in France where I remained for three years. Then I came home. My father and mother were very proud of my accomplishments. And I suppose I felt some pride myself. Pardonable vanity, I hope'.

'Certainly, my child. Continue please'.

'As I have already said my mother had high ambitions for me. She thought I should have the flower of the young men of the land at my feet to choose a husband from among them. Finally she cast her eye on a wealthy merchant in Kingscourt. He visited us a few times; and he invited us to his place in return. We were to go on a certain day and it was expected that he would ask for my hand on that occasion. He was a fine man. He was a sensible man. I liked him, but I did not love him. Sometimes I would ask myself was it right to give my hand to a man who didn't have my heart. I mentioned my worries to my mother. 'Childish nonsense', she replied. 'You like the man. You will be happy with him. Love will come afterwards. I know what I am talking about'.

'It was a fair day the day my mother took me to Kingscourt to settle my marriage. When we got into the town I heard a man singing, with a crowd gathered round him. I knew the man. I recognised him at once. I had met him a few years before that and imagined I was half in love with him. But then he left the country. He was on the road to a different career. In due course I stopped thinking about him. But when I saw him again and heard his voice the old love was rekindled, aye, burned with a fierce flame. I knew on the spot that I could never marry another man'.

'"Mamma", I said to my mother, "I prefer that we put off this visit until some other day"'.

"Why, child? What's wrong with you?" she asked anxiously.

'I told her I didn't feel well, that I felt as if I was going to faint – which wasn't altogether an untruth. There was a long argument. Finally we turned back and came home.

'The following year I got married to my wandering minstrel. My mother was inconsolable. I had disgraced her, she thought. Disgraced everyone belonging to her. Still it is due to her memory to say that we were never hungry while she was alive. Three years after I married she died. The following year my father died. He did not leave me a penny. The poor man had nothing to leave to anybody. The place was riddled with debts. For years they had been living above their means. That was perhaps one reason why mother wanted to marry me to the wealthy Kingscourt merchant.

'My love and I lived in a little cabin on the hillside a

few miles from where I was born and brought up. We struggled bravely for a while but the day came at last when we had to separate, each to fend for himself. I went out to look for work. I took every kind of employment that I could find. I imparted the rudiments of learning to a landlord's two young children. I taught French to a colonel's daughter. I made up their yearly accounts for small shopkeepers. I worked as a farm hand in County Meath and it makes me happy now to remember that during all the years I sent my darling every penny I could spare. I loved sending him money. Most people might find it hard to believe. But love and sacrifice are interchangeable terms. And, if I am not mistaken, that belief is one of the corner-stones of our Christian faith'.

'Pardon me for interrupting you', said the priest, 'but you are talking great stuff. It is no wonder that the man who had the heart of a child and the soul of a poet and the faith of a child, it is no wonder, I say, that such a man fell in love with you. But continue'.

'There is not much more to say. Two children we had – a boy and a girl. The girl died in infancy. The boy grew up to manhood and emigrated. We haven't heard from him for years. Maybe he is dead'.

She lapsed into silence.

'Where do you live now?' asked the priest, looking out at the falling snowflakes, as if he were anxious to know if the poor old woman had any place of shelter for the night.

'Over beyond Cashel', she replied. 'With a woman who has a houseful of children, one of them a young baby. I work there for my keep, as I have often done before'.

'My poor child, your lot in life has been a hard one', said the priest.

'I have had my moments of happiness, Father, and what those moments have meant to me the world does not understand. Most people that know me now and knew me when I was young think that the curse of heaven had fallen on me. As the old schoolmaster from Cavan town said last year, "Can it be possible that the two are the one and the same person – this old, withered, ugly hag and Molly Brady, once the fairest of Breffni's daughters?"'

'Molly Brady!' gasped the priest. 'Where did I hear that name? Ah! I remember it now. He mentioned it once in the college in Salamanca. I did not know who he married. So you are Molly Brady'.

'What is left of her, Father … I haven't long to go now and then we will be reunited in heaven never to part again … Many people thought Cathal Buí would never see heaven. Thought he was damned'.

'How wrong they were', said the priest.

'Well, they did think there was no coming back for him', said the old woman. 'My own mother thought it. And she was pious – genuinely pious. She was forever reading and quoting the Gospel. Yet there is one little incident in it that escaped her attention – the promise made to the penitent thief on Calvary'.

The priest felt a shudder going through his body. 'I too', said he, 'forgot an incident in the Gospel – the wedding in Cana'.

The funeral arrived at the old graveyard in Cashel. A grave had been dug beside the ruined abbey as Father O'Reilly had ordered. The coffin was lowered. Father O'Reilly read the burial service in a trembling voice.

The men filled in the grave. Then the priest, in a voice choking with emotion, spoke a few words. 'We have laid here the mortal remains of Cathal Buí McElgunn. Let us all hope and pray that on the day of the Resurrection we will be along with him and with the saint by whose side he wished to be buried. Good-bye, Cathal', said he, looking at the mound of earth that was already beginning to turn white.

And he walked away from the grave.

Notes

1 This is an English version of the story 'Ar Cheathramha Gheimhridh' which is published in *Fód a' Bháis* (An Gúm, 1955) 61-8.

2 Cathal Buí Mac Giolla Ghunna (1680-1756), a famous Gaelic poet identified with the counties of Fermanagh and Cavan. See, Robert Welch (ed.), *The Oxford Companion to Irish Literature* (OUP, 1996) 337.

3 *An Bonnán Buí* has been frequently translated by Thomas MacDonagh, James Stephens *et al.* Most recently and effectively it has been translated by Seamus Heaney and he can be heard reciting it on the CD *The Poet and the Piper* (Claddagh Records), a collaboration between this poet and the uilleann piper Liam O'Flynn.

THE SEA[1]

I know that after the events related in this story the rumour got abroad that I was doting. But it was a false rumour. I am not doting. It is only a little weakness - natural enough at my age. It occurs only at rare intervals. Sometimes when I am suddenly confronted with, or reminded of, a person or event associated with my childhood or youth, I forget the passage of time. The spell does not last long. As soon as it passes my mind and memory are as clear as ever.

Twenty-one years of age I was when I decided to go to America. The wanderlust was on me and I decided to go. But, eager as I was to travel and to see the world, it was not easy for me to leave my native Glenfadda. It was particularly hard to leave my parents. It was hard to part from the playmate of my childhood and youth - Neil McGilligan. Neil tried to persuade me to stay at home. He did his best to interest me in a pretty, little, dark-eyed girl that lived at the head of the glen. He was sure that if I were to fall in love I would not, could not, leave home. But you cannot fall in love just because someone wants you to. I was free from that tie and I was glad of it.

The few days before leaving I spent in visiting friends and relations and saying good-bye to them. That is what brought me all the way to Drumroe - a promontory that juts into the Atlantic from the coast of the Lower Rosses. I had a cousin married there. Drumroe is a narrow headland about a mile long. Its ridge is covered with brown heather. From its highest point there is a magnificent view - probably the finest in all Donegal, and that is saying something.

The day I visited Drumroe was a beautiful day in mid-summer. I walked out to the headland and I sat down. I was not long sitting when I heard someone singing. It was like the lilt of a bird. It was full of joy and gladness - the joy and gladness of childhood.

It was the voice of a little girl. She came to within about a dozen paces of me. Then she stood and looked at me as if she were puzzled, and she stopped singing. I looked at her from where I sat. And, as I did, she appeared to me to be the most beautiful thing that God had ever created. The thought struck me at once that if she were grown up, and that if she would consent to be mine, I would stay at home; and Neil McGilligan would have his wish when he least expected it. But she was only a child.

'Come over here and sit beside me', said I.

She did.

I looked at her again and I began talking to myself.

'Are you saying your prayers?' she asked me.

'No, child', I answered. 'I am reciting a poem that was in one of the lesson books when I was at school. You remind me of it. You are like the girl in the poem'.

'You, at school! A big man like you!'

'When I was a small boy', I explained.

'Say the poem for me'.

'I will. The part of it that applies to you. The verses that you remind me of'.

> I met a little cottage girl,
> She was eight years old, she said;
> Her hair was thick with many a curl
> That clustered round her head.
> She had a rustic, woodland air,
> And she was wildly clad;

Her eyes were fair, and very fair,
- Her beauty made me glad.

- 'We are Seven', W. Wordsworth

'I don't understand it', she said. 'I was only one day at school. I did not like the school. It was dark and dismal and ugly. I hated it. I wouldn't go back … But what is the meaning of your poem?'

I translated it into her vernacular as best I could.

'That is why you remind me of it', I added. 'Your beauty makes me glad'.

'Do you think I am beautiful?' she asked naively.

'I am certain of it, my child'.

'I am not as beautiful as the sea', she said. 'Do you know the sea?'

'I am afraid I don't. I was born and brought up away behind yonder blue mountain. This is my first time down here'.

'And when you were a small boy, there was no sea near you?'

'No sea near me'.

'Nor a strand to play on?'

'No strand to play on'.

'No sea and no strand. You have never seen the things I see down here on summer evenings'.

'And what do you see, child? Tell me all about it'.

'Well, yesterday evening I saw the Isle of the Blest. Away, away near the rim of the ocean. A beautiful island with tall forests and silver strands, and a harbour full of ships, and up on the height a huge palace, whiter than the newly-fallen snow'.

'So, you like the sea', I said when she had finished her description of the Isle of the Blest.

'I love the sea', she replied. 'And the sea loves me. When I am big I will earn lots of money and I will buy a boat. I will put a white sail on her - a sail whiter than the swan you see out there in the bay. I will go on board my boat and push her out from the shore, with a boathook, as the fishermen do. You push the rock and the boat moves out. Then I will hoist my white sail and I will sail away westward. Away beyond the sunset and to the Isle of the Blest. But I won't stay there. I will go to the end of the ocean and I will lay my hand on the glass wall of the sky. Then I'll come back home'.

'You won't stay in the Isle of the Blest?'

'Sure I must come back home to my granny'.

'You live with your granny, do you?'

'Yes, I do. And I must go home to her now or she will be out looking for me. She was putting the potatoes on the fire when I left. They must be boiled by now'.

She got up and she left me. I felt a sad loneliness come over me. I followed her with my eyes as she skipped across the headland towards her granny's little cabin. And then strange thoughts came into my head. What age would she be? About nine years, I estimated. In ten years more she would be nineteen!

Later on, I came to the house of my kinswoman whom I had included in my round of farewell visits. I could talk about nothing else but about the wonderful child I had met and about the things she had said to me.

'Some say she is under the spell of the fairies', said the man of the house. 'And at times I am inclined to believe it'.

'She had been badly reared', said my kinswoman. 'Allowed to grow up wild. This is the most of what is wrong with her. She is an orphan, the poor thing. Her mother died at the birth. The following year her father died - a cold he got and it went into consumption. The child has been brought up by the granny. Never went to school. Got her own way in everything. Just allowed to grow up wild'.

'Wild she may be', I said, 'but she is a wild beauty. There is poetry in every word that comes out of her mouth. She almost made me see the Isle of the Blest with its snow-white palace - away beyond the sunset'.

'It is a good thing you are going to America', said my kinswoman. 'If you were to meet her often she would turn your head. Then you'd be in a fix. There's hope for her: she is only a child. She may get sense when she grows up. You have all your sense got. If that were to be taken away from you, there would be no cure for you'.

The following evening Neil McGilligan and I were sitting on a heathery slope overlooking Glenfadda. It was our last evening together. 'Neil', I said, 'I have definitely decided to come back home in seven years' time'.

'That is good news', said Neil. 'When did you change your mind?'

'Yesterday evening when I was down in Drumroe', I replied.

II

But I did not come back in seven years' time as I had promised myself and others … Fifty years passed. And then I decided to make the journey.

Why did I decide to return to my native place after an absence of fifty years? Was it to see my parents? Of course not. My parents were long dead. All my relations were either dead or gone from the place. Strangers were living in the house I had been born and brought up in. My native Glenfadda would make me sad. Still, I wanted to come. And I would go down to Drumroe on a summer's evening, stand on the tip of the headland and look out towards the setting sun.

Strange to relate, during the voyage, Drumroe was in my mind more than my native Glenfadda. I often stood on the deck of the liner and looked out at the sea. There was no beauty in it. Just a ring of water meeting the sky at every point and only a short distance from the ship to the rim of the circle. No, I thought to myself, there is no beauty in the sea except when seen from the land. When seen from a place like Drumroe. And to Drumroe I would go.

Would I meet her whose beauty made me glad when I was a young man and she a little child? Was she alive? What would I say to her? Would she remember me? … Perhaps she had written great poetry. Perhaps her name was a household word from end to end of the country. Then I remembered that she had never gone to school and could neither read nor write … Maybe she composed poetry in her native language – the language most fit to give expression to her weird imagery. Of course, that language would not make her known. Her native tongue was gone from the country.

In due course I arrived at the nearest village to my native place. I put up at the hotel. Nobody knew me. Nobody was interested in me. I was an American come to spend a holiday in Ireland; that was all. After a few days I went to Glenfadda. Nobody there knew me. As I have said, strangers were living in what had once been my home.

At last I enquired if a man named Neil McGilligan lived in the Glen. I was told there was such a man and his house was pointed out to me. I went to see him. He was in bed, sick. I told him who I was. I thought he would be glad to see me. I reminded him of the time we had together when we were young. He was not interested. He had suffered much and there was no hope of his recovery. He seemed vexed with me because I was alive and well and he dying.

However, I would go to Drumroe. I had never forgotten that most beautiful spot. I had seen it in my mind's eye now and again during half a century.

The following day I went there. It was a beautiful summer day. Exactly like the day I had been there fifty years before. The headland was the same. The heather blossom had the same colour. Nothing had changed. I looked towards the western horizon. Somewhere out there, I thought, the Isle of the Blest is located.

And the girl whose beauty had made me glad? She too was there. She came tripping across the headland. When she was within a few yards of me she stood and looked at me.

There she was with her big, dreamy, blue eyes and her golden ringlets. I beckoned to her. She came to me and sat beside me, without the slightest hesitation.

'The sea is beautiful again today', said I.

'I don't like the sea', she replied.

'Why? What has happened?'

'I don't like the sea. I hate it. The sea is bad and cruel'.

'So, you have changed your mind all of a sudden! You won't buy a boat when you have grown up. You won't put a white sail on it – whiter than the neck of the swan – and sail away to the Isle of the Blest, and from there to the glass wall of the sky where it dips into the ocean'.

She looked at me with eyes full of wonder.

'I don't understand you, sir', she said nervously.

'But you told me yesterday you would buy a boat when you grew up. What made you change your mind so suddenly?'

'Yesterday? I wasn't down here yesterday'.

'Don't you remember? Ah, you do. We were sitting here where we are now'.

'I haven't been down here for the past four or five days. It must have been some other girl you met. I know now who she was. See that long, white house up on the height. There is a girl in that house the same age as me. She is like me too. Must have been her you met. She comes down here every day. She doesn't hate the sea as I hate it … I must go and take my granny home'.

'Where is your granny?' I asked.

'Sitting over beyond that rock', answered the girl. 'She often comes down there and she sits and cries. Sometimes, when she is tired crying, she falls asleep. I must go and bring her home. But it is very strange'.

'What is strange, child?'

'What you have said to me about buying a boat and putting a snow-white sail on her and sailing away to the Isle of the Blest. They say granny used to talk like that when she was a girl like I am now. It was Shamey More I heard saying it. The old man that lives in yon house over the far cliff'.

Like a lightning flash my illusion vanished and my memory came back to me.

'Do you mind if I go along with you to see your granny?' said I.

'You may come if you like', replied the girl, 'but she mightn't talk to you. Sometimes, on an evening like this, she talks to nobody'.

III

I went along with the little girl to where her granny sat, behind a boulder, on a ledge overlooking the sea. The old woman was not crying but she was the living image of sadness and sorrow. Her face was withered and wrinkled. Her eyes were small and sunken. And her white hair was scattered in wisps down her neck and shoulders.

I had decided that I would not remind her of her childhood days too abruptly. I would lead round to it gradually.

'The blessing of God on you, my good woman', I said. 'You are admiring the scenery'.

'I am admiring nothing', she replied in a mournful voice. 'Just looking straight in front of me and nothing to meet my eye but the sea'.

'Even the sea', I said, 'it is beautiful no matter where you see it from. And, from where you sit, it is just heavenly'.

'The beauty of the sea', replied the old woman. 'I see no beauty in her cruel, wicked face. And what do I see as I look out from where I sit? I see the bleached bones of my babies tossed on the breakers as they roll in towards the strand … Ah, if you only knew the sea as I know her. But you don't. You have never had any dealings with her. You have come down here sight-seeing, like many another, I suppose. You looked out at the sea and found her beautiful. She looked back at you and smiled the smile of an angel at you. But it is like the smile and the beauty of a wicked woman who would plunge your soul into hell's lake of burning brimstone'.

I did not, of course, understand the meaning of half of what she had said. But she continued.

'The malice and wickedness of the sea. Talk about the serpent hidden under an innocent-looking flower, as Billy More the *seanchaí* used to say ... You don't understand. There was a time when I didn't understand either. When I would fight with anyone that would say a hard word against the sea. When I was a little girl – about the same age and size as that girl there – I thought there was nothing in the world as beautiful as the sea, or as good. I used to sit here and look across to the outer rim of the ocean. I used to day-dream of the life I'd have when I grew up. I would buy a boat and rig her out with snow-white sails. I would sail away westward. Away beyond the sunset until I'd lay my hand on the glass wall of the dome of the sky. I loved the sea at the time. And I thought the sea loved me. She was as quiet and gentle as a lamb. Little did I dream that the day would come when the gentle lamb would become a raging lion and devour the children of my womb and their father along with them'.

She became silent for a little while as if she were trying to overcome her emotion. Then she began again.

'Oh, the cruel, wicked sea. She snatched away my man and my three sons and my little grandson. My poor husband. He thought there wasn't as much water as would drown him between the Needle of the Foreland and the Stags of Aran. One fine summer evening he went out in his curragh to lift lobster-pots. There wasn't a breath of wind out. The sea was as calm as a pond. I was listening to the lilt of his song as he went down the bay. Just as he was crossing the Red Reef she broke – what had never been known to happen in settled weather. His little craft was swamped and smothered in a whirlpool of seething surf … Years afterwards two of my sons and a grandson were drowned the same way. In both cases the wicked sea struck as sudden as a lightning flash. My two sons, Neil and Manus, were going to Inishfree for a cargo of kelp. Neil took his little son with him – a lad of four years. The day was dead calm. The weather was settled. They carried no ballast. Thought there was no need for it. When they were in the middle of the sound, a sudden squall struck them. The boat capsised immediately. The three were drowned. A week later, the child's body was washed ashore at Traderg. The bodies of the other two were never found'.

'It was then that my remaining son, Murty, the father of that girl there, it was then that he decided to have no more dealings with the sea. He sold the boat. But the sea got him. Nothing less than a clean sweep of my children would satisfy her. One day Murty was walking along the strand at the foot of a cliff. He was more than twenty yards from the water's edge. A big wave rolled in out of nowhere and knocked him against the face of the cliff. He fell down stunned. The wave lifted him up on her bosom and carried him out to the deep where he was drowned. Oh, God of heaven!' she exclaimed, and she burst out crying.

'But', said she, after a pause, 'the sea can't take any more of my men folk from me. She has them all. I have no more left. No husband, no son, no grandson. All gone'.

'It is a sad tale, my poor woman', said I. 'And I am sorry if I have added to your distress by mentioning the beauty of the sea. But when I did so, I did not know your sad story'.

'How could you know?' said she, recovering somewhat. 'How could any stranger know? … You are American, aren't you, if it is no harm to ask?'

'I am not American born', I replied. 'But I have been in that country for fifty years. I was born and brought up in a place called Glenfadda, away beyond yon ridge of blue hills'.

'Glenfadda', said she. 'I heard the name. I met a man from that place long ago when I was a little girl. He had a cousin married down here. He came to see her one day. That was the day I met him. He recited verses from a schoolbook for me. I told him all about the boat I was going to buy. He did not laugh at my childhood nonsense. He looked sad. He said he would come back some day and sail to the Isle of the Blest along with me. But I never saw him again afterwards'.

I did not tell her who I was. What would be the use?

Note

1   This is an English version of the story 'An Fhairrge' which is published in *Tráigh is Tuile* (An Gúm, 1955) 110-6.

A Queen's Taboo[1]

I had just come home having completed my studies in a teachers' training college and I was offered a school in Inishmore – an island about two miles from the coast of the Rosses of Donegal.

'It is the best I can do for you at the present', said the parish priest to me. 'In due course you will get a school on the mainland; but you must wait till it comes to your turn. And now, be careful! Never try to navigate the sound on your own. It is full of sunken reefs. But most times you will get a passage to the mainland on Saturday … Are you fond of reading? … Very good. An island is just the place for a young man who wants to read and study'.

'Would you have any idea, Father, where on the island I could get digs?'

'I was coming to that', replied the priest. 'You will get digs with the Queen, and very good digs too. Nobody in the house but herself. You will be very well looked after'.

'The Queen! Did you say I was to stay with a queen, Father?'

'Yes, with a queen. But don't run away with any hasty notions. You will never be a king. Nor will any of your children inherit a throne. That dynasty is nearing its end. It will die out with the present monarch. The Queen is over sixty years of age and a widow. Her only child, a daughter, is married on the mainland'.

'And why is she called the Queen, Father?'

'Some old custom that, they say, goes back for over a thousand years. I don't know the origin of it. I suppose nobody does. But they call her the Queen.[2] And, would you believe it, I always imagine there is something queenly about her. Some strain of royalty or nobility. A 'nobility that doth hedge a king', as old Bill has it …[3] Quite a few teachers have stayed with her since I became manager of that school. They were all loud in praise of her except one. He got into trouble - serious trouble - and he blamed the Queen for it. Said she acted out of malice. But I could never believe it. There was a misunderstanding somewhere. At least, that is my opinion. Nothing can make me believe that there is the least malice in the same queen. The most that can be said is that she did not give the teacher what he would consider a satisfactory explanation. But failure to give a satisfactory explanation does not in itself constitute a crime'.

I went to the island and got digs with the Queen. I liked her from the moment I met her. The day I came she told me she was glad to have a boarder that could talk to her in her own language.

She was like a mother to me. She was more than solicitous for my welfare. If I happened to come in with my clothes damp, after a shower, she would not let me sit down until I had changed into dry ones. On one occasion I got sick and had to stay in bed for a week. The Queen minded me as well as any trained nurse would. She was efficient. She was kind and gentle. She was dignified.

Often, on winter evenings, we sat one on each side of the fire, the Queen knitting, I reading, with my back to the wall lamp. The Queen would never speak until I put down my book and lit my pipe. Then she would begin and she certainly was worth listening to. She had a fund of folklore that was truly amazing.

I will never forget her as I saw her and listened to her one winter's night. The little kitchen was warm and comfortable. The fire burned cheerfully on the hearth. The lamp shone on the sanded floor and on the delf on the dresser. The wind howled in the chimney; and I could hear the breakers against the cliffs of the shore.

The Queen excelled herself that night. At times I felt that she had put a magic spell on me. She was young again, in all the bloom of her beauty ... She was Niamh of the Golden Hair and I was Oisin. She was taking me away on her snow-white steed, over thousands of miles of ocean, to the Land of Perpetual Youth ... I sat spellbound listening to her.

'I must get up and get a bit of supper for you, master', she said at last. 'It is getting late'.

'One second, please', I pleaded. 'Is it any harm to ask you why you are called the Queen?'

'I am called the Queen because I am a queen', she replied. 'Just as my father was called the King. The royal line goes back over twelve hundred years. The first sovereign of this island was crowned by Colmcille. On that rock you see on the height in the middle of the island. It was there that Colmcille blessed my ancestor and put the white wand of kingship in his hand ... But I am the last of that line of monarchs. I had only one child - a daughter. She is married on the mainland. The line is nearing its end', she said, sadly. And she blinked a few times, as if tears were gathering in her eyes.

Some weeks afterwards I happened to be in Letterkenny one Saturday, attending one of those dreary functions known as teachers' meetings. After the meeting a man came to me and introduced himself.

'You are in Inishmore', said he.

I replied that I was.

'And staying with the Queen?'

'Yes, staying with the Queen'.

'I taught on that God-forsaken rock for three years, and I stayed with the same Queen, as they call her. Sorry I did not meet you before you went to the island. I'd have advised you to look for digs in some other house. I could have given you the benefit of my own bitter experience of the Queen. I would have warned you to keep away from her'.

'The Queen is a grand woman', I protested. 'She is kind and generous and courteous'.

'And therein lies the danger. She looks the innocent flower and she is the serpent under it, as the man said. For over two years I thought she was an angel. Little did I dream that all the time she was nursing her venom in her cruel heart and only waiting for an opportunity to ruin me'.

'But why should she?'

'I am sure I don't know. Never tried to find out her motive. Only telling you what happened … Yes, she was nice and kind and gentle to all appearances ever until she saw her chance. Then she struck. She contrived to have me dismissed and would have succeeded only Father Brennan, the manager, took my part. And a tough battle he had to fight to save me. For the evidence against me was damning. And it was all contrived by Her Majesty, the Queen of Inishmore'.

'Pardon me for saying it', I broke in, 'but I am afraid I am going to find it difficult to believe that your estimation of the Queen is correct'.

'Listen to my story then', he continued. 'One night, I went across to Benaroan where some of the islanders were making poteen. I spent the greater part of the night in the still-house. (For what else could a man do at times in such a God-forsaken hole?) It was near morning when I came back to the digs. The fire was burning brightly on the hearth and the table set beside it. The Queen heard me coming in and she got up to get me something to eat. I told her to get back to bed for that I could not look at food (which was the truth, for the damned stuff had burned the stomach out of me). As she was leaving the kitchen I warned her to be sure and call me in time for school. I knew there was the danger that I'd sleep it out after the booze. At another time this would not worry me too much. I knew the inspector was in Dungloe. I had got the signal from the mainland the day before - the red flag on a pole in Illanbo. Well, I went to bed and fell asleep. When I woke in the morning I had a feeling that it was late. I made one grab at my watch. It was within a few minutes of twelve o'clock. I jumped out of bed at once and dressed. I ran to the schoolhouse. The children were huddled together in a corner of the yard and the inspector doing guard over them. He would not let any of them leave in case I'd get word that he was there.

'The report was made, the enquiry followed. As I have told you, I'd have been dismissed only the manager put all he knew into defending me ... I asked the Queen afterwards why she didn't call me in time for school. She said she would not call anybody out of his sleep in the morning. As you probably know, she does not speak English too well. So she lapsed into her own lingo. She delivered herself of a long rigmarole nine tenths of which was Greek to me. All I could make out was that there was a *geas* on her and that she was not allowed to call anyone in the morning. I don't know what the *geas* is … A name for some kind of diabolic wickedness that is hidden in her black heart … That is the Queen of Inishmore for you. Every word of what I have told you is true. So, be on your guard, my young man'.

I did not, of course, believe that there was the slightest malice in the Queen. The most that could be said of her was that she imagined herself to be under a *geas* that would not allow her to call anyone in the morning. Even of this I was not sure and, before I could make up my mind, I should require further proof.

I decided to put the matter to the test. One Friday evening I told the Queen that I intended to go to the mainland in the morning in one of the island boats. The boat, I told her, would leave around eight o'clock so as to be past the bar before the tide turned.

'Call me about a quarter past seven', I said.

'Don't depend on me, master', said the Queen. 'I am a very heavy sleeper at times, especially in the morning. Perhaps because I don't sleep when I go to bed. The rheumatism keeps me awake. I have it again this week. So don't depend on me to call you'.

That was one truth established. I was certain it was taboo for the Queen to call a person in the morning. But what was the reason for this taboo? Was it a traditional obligation imposed on her as monarch of her little kingdom? There was mention of similar taboos in the old legends. One of the chieftains of the Red Branch could not refuse an invitation to a banquet. It was this *geas* that compelled him to go to Barach's feast and abandon the sons of Uisneach to the treachery of Conor mac Neasa. The Fianna were subject to similar *geasa*. Fionn could not refuse a request asked of him by a woman. Goll's taboo was the direct opposite: he could not grant a woman's request. The Queen of Inishmore could not call a person in the morning. Had this *geas* come down from the first coronation on the island, notwithstanding the fact that Colmcille himself blessed it?

I was very curious to know. But how could I find out? I decided to ask the Queen the first opportunity I should get. One evening when she was in her best story-telling humour, I made up my mind to ask her about the meaning and origin of the taboo. She must have sensed what was in my mind for every time I tried to lead up to the question I wanted to ask, she headed me off in another direction. In the end I concluded it was useless to ask her. She was good to me. She was kind to me. But she was a queen and I was only a plebeian. I was not entitled to know royal secrets.

III

One fine Saturday afternoon in July I met Black Murtach.

'Master', said he, 'we are going out to fish for pollock; would you care to come? I'll fix up a line and hook for you. There's no great art in pollock-fishing. Just let your line float in the wake of the boat. When you get the bite, you will give a wee tug to fix the hook firmly in your fish. Then you'll pull hand over hand for all you're worth. That's all that's in it'.

I decided to try my hand. Shortly afterwards all was ready and we set out from the west pier. Black Murtach was at the helm.

'We'll run across to the Clutches', said he. 'From there we'll go straight to the Stags … It should be a good evening for pollock-fishing - a calm sea, a nice sailing breeze but not too strong'.

I noticed that Black Murtach looked back over his shoulder at frequent intervals. I noticed also that he was not steering straight for the Clutches although the breeze was blowing in that direction. I asked him why he was going out of his way.

'Do you want to drown the whole lot of us?' said he. 'You don't know that Death may be lying in wait for us on the straight line from Inishmore to the Clutches. But I'll make a seaman of you, master, before you leave the island. If you went on a straight line from the west pier to the Clutches, you would sail right across the Blower. And, let me tell you, if the Blower happened to blow up under you, you would not sail across her a second time'.

'What is the Blower?' I asked.

'A sunken reef', replied Black Murtach. 'She could break any time. You don't know the day nor the hour. It is three months now since she broke. But the danger is there all the time'.

'Would it break on a day like today? Sure the sea is as calm as a duck pond'.

'True for you, master. But she could break on a calm day as well as on a stormy day. It is the strange way that the groundswell works. First there comes a hollow as if the bed of the ocean had cracked open and the water had gone down through it. Then the sea rushes in on all sides to fill the hollow. It rushes with such force that a big mountain of water shoots up, with a peak on it like Errigal. Then it breaks at the top and rolls back on all sides. It would swamp the Glasgow steamer, not to say a small fishing boat'.

'And how exactly do you know where it is since it cannot be seen until it breaks?'

'We have landmarks that will take us clear of her. That is why I look back from time to time. Going out from the west pier you keep Carricknarone covering the light of Torglass. That will bring you on a line about fifty yards to the east of the Blower. And you need fifty yards to keep clear of the suction'.

'Was there ever a boat lost on the Blower?'

'Alas, there was. A boat from our island. Forty years ago it happened. Forty years next Saturday to be exact. A crew from the island - four of them - were going out to fish for pollock just as we are going now, God save us and guard us! The weather was settled. The sea was dead calm. The Blower hadn't broken for three months before that. The men thought there wasn't the slightest danger. They decided to take the shortcut to the Clutches. Just as they were on top of the Blower, she burst up. The whole four of them were drowned. The boat was smashed to splinters ... That was the sad day for our island'.

'I've never heard about it'.

'Strange that the Queen never mentioned it to you', said Black Murtach. 'Her own husband – Red Godfrey O'Donnell – was one of the four men drowned that day. I remember it well. I was only a youth at the time. It was four days afterwards that we found poor Godfrey O'Donnell's body wedged in between two rocks in Magheranagall. God save us, I'll never forget it. His face was battered and broken and his teeth smashed in. That was the sad day. And the way it happened ... Two or three minutes in seven months. And in that short space of time four fine young lives were lost. The poor Queen nearly lost her reason. In fact, she did lose it for a spell. For several days she went about tearing her hair and

saying that she had murdered her husband. But thank
God she recovered gradually'.

IV

The following Saturday I got up late. I came into the
kitchen. The fire was still raked. The Queen was sitting on
a low stool in the chimney corner, her hair uncombed, her
shoes unlaced. Her face was tear-stained and there was a
look of dreadful anguish in her eyes.

'Are you ill, Queen?' I asked her.

She burst into tears. For about five minutes she wept
bitterly. Her whole frame shook and all she could say
was: 'O, my God, why did I do it? Why did I do it? What
wicked curse fell on me that fatal morning? Where was
God's holy mother? Why didn't she come and stand
between me and the wickedness and snares of the devil?'

Her grief, which seemed to border on despair, if not
on madness, wrung my heart, and I tried to console her
as best I could.

'Don't cry, Queen', I said. 'Tell me what has happened
you. Whatever it is, don't bear the weight of it on
yourself. Try to stop crying and tell me. It will bring you
some relief'.

She stopped crying.

'Pardon me, master', said she, 'I should have your
breakfast ready for you. And here I am with nothing
done – the fire not even lit. But I couldn't help it. I
couldn't, master. This day of the year never comes round
but it tears and tortures the very heart within me. This
day forty years my poor husband, Lord have mercy on
him, was drowned. O, God, when I think of it. But you

61

never heard the story, master. You don't understand my sorrow'.

'I did hear of it', I said. 'Black Murtach told me all about the drowning last Saturday'.

'He did not tell you all, master', she sobbed. 'He doesn't know it all. Nobody but myself knows it. For forty years I have kept the terrible story to myself. But this morning I felt that I had to tell it or my heart would break. It is a frightful story … Ah, I cannot tell you, much as I want to. I cannot'.

'Ah, do, Queen, tell me if it relieves your mind'.

She paused for a few seconds. Then she spat out the words as if they had been burning her mouth. 'I was the cause of my husband's death … There now. It is out at last'.

'I must tell it from the beginning', she resumed after a pause. 'You have heard of the Blower, master. Sometimes she doesn't break for months. And then, all of a sudden, in the calmest of weather perhaps, she bursts all of a sudden and shoots a pillar of water into the sky. When it breaks and falls down it would swamp everything within two hundred yards of it. Well, one fine summer evening my husband and three other men from the island decided to go out fishing for pollock the following morning. When we were going to bed that night he told me he'd have to be up early in the morning as they wanted to get away before the tide turned. I got up at sunrise. I kindled the fire and hung on the kettle. When the breakfast was ready I went into the bedroom and called him. I think I see him yet as he was at that moment, with his red, curly hair and beard, as he lay asleep on the pillow. I shook him by the shoulder and told him it was time for him to get up. He opened his eyes and said he would. I came back to the kitchen. Five minutes passed and not a stir out of him. I went into the bedroom a second time and called him. He looked up at me this time in a strange way. (It was only afterwards I understood that look – pleading to be allowed to sleep on). He said he was getting up immediately. I came back to the kitchen again. Ten more minutes passed and not a sound or a stir in the bedroom. I went to the window and looked out. And there was the boat and the rest of the crew down at the creek waiting for him. I went to the bedroom a third time. He had gone to sleep again. I caught him by the shoulder and shook him. And, O Blessed Mother of God, the words I said to him: 'Look here', I said, 'either you are getting up or you are not. The tide won't wait for you'.

'He jumped out of bed and dressed and came down to the kitchen. He took his breakfast and was in the best of humour. He did not in the least mind what I had said to him ... He collected his fishing lines and went out. I was standing at the door looking after him. That was the last time I saw him alive – just as he was running down to the pier ... We were only married a year at the time. One short year. Our baby was five weeks old'.

She paused. I wanted her to continue.

'How did it happen?' I asked, as if I did not know the details. 'A sudden storm?'

'There was no storm', replied the Queen. 'The weather was settled, the sea dead calm. They were going to the Clutches and they took the shortcut. The Blower hadn't broken for three months before. They thought they were safe. When they were on top of the reef, she blew up. All four of them were drowned ... Poor Godfrey! I often asked myself what were his thoughts when he saw the frightful mountain of water falling to bits and pouring down on them ... His body was the last to be recovered. Four days afterwards they found him at the foot of the cliffs at Magheranagall, wedged in between two rocks. They carried him on a door-leaf across the island and brought him in and laid him on that floor. His hair and beard had turned dark and seemed glued to his head and face ... How I kept my reason, I don't know. I suppose God took pity on my poor, innocent baby. I deserved no pity'.

'You did, Queen. It was for you God had the pity'.

'But, when I think of it', she resumed, 'the Blower hadn't broken for three months. Didn't break for four months afterwards. Three or four minutes in seven months. And, in that flash of time, my poor man was drowned. A few minutes later and she would have blown up before they reached her. But I called him! I called him sternly. I made him get up in time for his doom. I told him the tide wouldn't wait for him ... And the sleep that was on him that morning! As if he felt he should sleep until the moment of danger was past ... When he didn't get up the second time, I called him. Why didn't I take that as a warning? ... Why didn't it occur to me that I shouldn't have called him at all – the first time any more than the third time? Why didn't I realise that Death may be lying in wait for a person and that it could be avoided by letting him sleep until the hour of danger was past?'

And she burst out crying again.

Notes
1   This is an English version of the story 'Geis na Bainríoghaine' which is published in *Fallaing Shíoda* (An Gúm, 1956) 92-8.
2   It is well-established that there were 'kings' on some of the larger islands of Ireland e.g. most famously on the Great Blasket, in Co. Kerry, and on Tory Island, in Co. Donegal. It is also attested that there was a 'queen', Mary Herritty, on Tory

Island. There is a death note for her published in the *Irish Independent* (22.2.36, 7).

3   The author frequently inserts lines from Shakespeare's plays in the English versions of his stories.

An American I Met[1]

It is my own fault or perhaps failing. Whatever you like to call it, it is there and I cannot help it. I don't like meeting strangers. People often tell me that I could overcome this unsociable inclination. Perhaps I could at one time. But it is too late now.

The fact remains that I do not like talking to strangers. That is why I go to a quiet place every year for my holidays. That is why I went to Rossdaragh last year. Rossdaragh has everything that I desire. It is on the edge of the sea (and I love the sea). It has a good, comfortable hotel. There are never many visitors there. Young people avoid it. It is too quiet for them and too lonely. They prefer the crowds and the dance-halls, in places like Salthill and Bundoran.

Last August I went to Rossdaragh for my holidays. There were only a few visitors staying at the hotel, for which I was glad. One man tried to talk to me the day I arrived. But he soon gave it up. I expect he concluded I was a stupid old stick not worth bothering with. After the first day he left me severely alone.

On the evening of the third day I was sitting on a bench in front of the hotel, looking dreamingly across the bay to Portnoo. A car came up the drive and stopped within a few yards of where I sat. The occupants alighted. There was no mistaking their nationality: they were American. You could recognise it at once. You would know it from the size and make of their car. You would know it by their accent and by the way they gave orders to the porter. It was something, I thought, to be a citizen of the most powerful nation in the world.

They were three in number - a middle-aged man, a woman somewhat younger in appearance, and a boy of about twelve years. I guessed that they were husband and wife and their son. My guess turned out to be right.

The man wanted to talk to everybody. He seemed particularly bent on talking to me. At breakfast the first morning they were at the table next to me. The man began talking to me. I did not tell him straight out that I did not want to make his acquaintance, but I went as near to it as anyone could without being positively rude. After three or four attempts, he gave up. And I was glad. I said to myself that he must have understood that I did not want his conversation.

But I was not finished with him. After breakfast I went out and down to the top of the cliffs overlooking the Atlantic. I looked around for a cosy spot and, having found one, I sat down and lit my pipe. After about a quarter of an hour the American came down and his son along with him. The boy had his own pastime: he began to fling pebbles into the sea. The father came to where I sat and stood beside me.

He began talking to me. The scenery from Rossdaragh, he said, was just superb. In fact, the whole county was beautiful. But its roads, he said, were a downright disgrace to any country that claimed to be civilised. He had nearly got into trouble the day before. His car, he said, went within an ace of turning right over. And judging by his description of the place and the way he had come, I concluded that it was at the Doochary Corkscrews he had been in trouble.

He sat down beside me and pulled out his pipe. How under heaven was I going to shake him off?

'What kind of tobacco do you smoke?' he asked.

'Black plug', I replied.

'Vile stuff', said he. 'Tried it once when I couldn't get anything else. It was in Dublin. Part of my luggage had gone astray. I couldn't do without a smoke, of course. I bought a bit of your black plug. It nearly killed me'.

'It is all right when you get used to it', said I. 'And it has the advantage of being cheap'.

He handed me his pouch and asked me if I cared to try a fill of American tobacco. I could not very well refuse his offer. I filled my pipe and lit it. The tobacco was good. I said so but I could not stop talking at that. When a man gives you a fill of tobacco and you accept it, you can't refuse to talk to him. I had to say something. But what would I talk about? I know next to nothing about America and he could not be expected to know much about Ireland. At last I decided to get him to talk about his boy. Parents like to tell you about their children. All you have to do is to listen. I asked him how the boy was getting on at school.

He told me a lot about classes and forms and high school. The most of it was Greek to me but I had to say something. At last I thought of a topic that was very much in the news in our own country - corporal punishment in school. I asked him if the children were slapped in American schools.

'Of course they are when they misbehave', he replied. 'How else could you run a school? Sure if children weren't afraid of the rod, they would go wild - especially the boys'.

'But are they punished for failing in their lessons?' I asked.

'For failing in their lessons?' he said, and he looked at me in amazement. 'What put that into your head? Do you think America is a land of lunatics? If you want to prevent a child from learning, to make it really stupid if it is not so already, start putting knowledge into it with a rod ... I know your country has a proud title among the nations of the world - the Isle of Saints and Scholars. But you must give us Americans credit for at least that bit of common sense'.

I was left with nothing more to say and I made some excuse to get away from him.

'Fill your pipe again before you go', said he. 'And if you like that tobacco I have plenty of it - as much as will keep the two of us smoking for weeks'.

I went away disgusted with myself for having fallen so stupidly into his trap. Why didn't I say at the beginning that I did not like American tobacco? That I had tried it once and that it burned my mouth and throat? Now I was caught and had no excuse. What was I to do? He had evidently made up his mind to force himself and his tobacco on me. For the rest of the day I managed to avoid him. After lunch I went to my bedroom and I remained there until I saw himself and his wife, with their son, drive away in their car.

II

That night, when I went to bed, I began to try to invent a plan that would rid me of this annoying foreigner. I decided to have somewhere to go every day. I had noticed that he had no fishing gear in his car the day he came. Supposing I were to borrow a rod from the proprietor of the hotel and go out in the direction of the lakes every day that was fine. I would lie there for hours in the heather. But I could not avoid him at meal-time and he would be offering me tobacco. How could I combat that? The first plan that suggested itself to me was to say that I could not continue to smoke another man's tobacco. But I rejected that as being too crude. Then it occurred to me to say that after a day or two American tobacco did not agree with me - that it gave me indigestion. But what if he had a remedy for that? A small white tablet to be taken after each smoke. Just for four or five days. Then the stomach upset would ... It was a characteristic of all good tobacco etc. etc ... It was tough luck, I thought, that in a country that was supposed to be free a man could not spend a hard-earned holiday without being pestered by foreigners.

After a time I began to think about what the American had said about corporal punishment in schools. If schoolchildren misbehaved they must be punished for it. How else could one run a school? If they weren't afraid of the rod, they would go wild. And then what he had said about corporal punishment for failure to learn: 'If you want to prevent a child from learning, to make it really stupid if it is not so already, start putting knowledge into it with a rod'.

I hope, I said to myself, he doesn't find out. I hope he does not remain long enough in Ireland to find out that when Johnny became Seán and Ned became Éamann and Frank became Proinsias, they proceeded, by means of the rod, to revive a dead language, to give the nation a new vernacular!

Corporal punishment in schools! The thought brought me back to the few years of my life I had spent teaching. The old school in Lettercagh came vividly before me. I saw the window from which I used to watch for the signal announcing the coming of the inspector. I saw the children sitting in the desks before me. I recalled some of their names and their faces.

I began to examine my conscience. When I was a teacher, did I ever slap the children? An odd time, I had to admit to myself. Did I ever try to put knowledge into them with a rod? No, I did not. I had nothing to accuse myself of on that score. Did I ever lose my temper and punish a child more severely than I ought to have done, or would have done had I kept cool? That was a sore point. I had to admit to myself that I had been guilty on one occasion. And the whole episode came back to me.

III

It happened in this way. In those days the bigger boys used to hire with the farmers of the Lagan for the summer season and come to school only while they were at home in the winter. Among these migratory birds was a boy named Michael O'Donnell. Michael was a big, strong, hardy lad and full of devilment. He was learning nothing at school, not because he was lacking in intelligence but because he did not want to learn. More than once I told him that it would be better for him, and much better for me, and for the school, if he were to stay at home. For he was a constant source of disturbance. He was a hero to the rest of the boys and they wanted to imitate him. Consequently, he had far greater influence over them than I had.

He was stultifying my best efforts at teaching and was making my position as principal of the school ridiculous. One day I commanded him to hold out his hand to be slapped. He said he would not and he looked at me with defiance in his eye. I made a swipe at him. He jumped sideways and my fist shot harmlessly past his shoulder. I tried again and again, but he always managed to side-step me. I had never seen such expert footwork, nor never read of such (with the possible exception of Jim Corbett). In the end, he had me in such a state of mind that I had to give up. I did no teaching that day.

One day I complained to his father about him. 'Keep him at home, Séamas', I pleaded. 'Get something for him to do, if it were only opening a bog drain and closing it again. He'll never learn anything at school. You can take that from me'.

'You needn't tell me that, master. I know he won't learn anything at school. Yet I think he is very intelligent. He has a powerful memory'.

'And why can I never get him to learn even one verse of a poem in his reader?'

'I don't know, master. But I know he has a powerful memory. You should hear him singing 'Brennan on the Moor' and 'Willy Reilly and His Colleen Bawn' and 'Moorloch Mary' and 'The Risin' of the Moon' and scores of such songs. Of course I know he is full of devilment and that he is upsetting your school. But I also know that he is full of good nature'.

'You admit, Séamas, that he is full of devilment and that he will never learn anything from his teacher. Then why send him to school?'

'I am not sending him to school to learn, master. It is just that he is a bit wild at the moment and I want you to put some manners on him'.

'But how, Séamas?'

'Give him the rod, plenty of the rod'.

'I don't like doing that. I would not like any child in my school to grow up with a spite against me'.

'When our Michael grows up, master, he'll have no spite against you – if I know him'.

One day, as I was calling the roll, I heard sounds of muffled laughter coming from the far end of the room.

'Silence!' I shouted, without looking up from the roll-book.

'Silence, I say, so that I can hear you answer your names ... Michael O'Donnell, I know you are the cause of it all. But, if I have to go down to you, you'll be sorry for yourself. I'll beat you to within an inch of your life'.

There was a louder outburst of laughter. I looked down and there was Michael O'Donnell, smoking a pipe for all he was worth. He was pulling very hard at it. A cloud of smoke was rising towards the ceiling and curling out through the open window.

I felt that the crisis in my professional career had come. I must act and act quickly. I had to do one of two things: either acknowledge myself defeated and resign my post or come to grips with open rebellion. At the same time I did not want to hurt the boy more than was necessary. I would not smash his jaw bone or knock in his front teeth unless I were forced to do so in self-defence. But that too was a possibility to be reckoned with.

I had some slight knowledge and experience of boxing and I decided to make whatever use I could of it. I rushed down to Michael O'Donnell and made a feint at him with my right. He side-stepped as usual and, as he did so, he walked into where my left was aimed at. It was not a very heavy blow (I will say that much for myself) but he got it on the side of the head. He turned round as if he meant to run away and get out into the open where he could use his footwork with more advantage. Then he tripped on a satchel that someone had let fall on the floor and he fell on his face. A short tin whistle and two rusty nails fell from his inside pocket onto the floor. A piece of twine was hanging out of another pocket. There was a rent on the seat of his pants.

These were the little things that got me. A sudden wave of remorse overwhelmed me. I felt my stomach heaving … I knew that in a few years' time he would be a grown man and would have his own back at me. But it was not that that worried me. No, it was the realisation that I had hit a child with my fist and knocked him down. For what else was he but a child? The proofs of his childhood were there before my eyes. The tin whistle, the nails and the piece of twine - a child's little playthings accusing me before God.

I finished calling the roll and chalked up the attendance. Michael O'Donnell was sitting in one of the back desks sullenly contemplating his fingernails. If he only knew how sorry I am, I thought. But I cannot tell him. He would ride roughshod over the whole school. I looked out the window and my heart missed a beat. There was the signal on Paddy Davy's Height - a red handkerchief flying from the shaft of a spade. The inspector was on his way from Dungloe.

In due course he arrived. He looked round the schoolroom. Michael O'Donnell was sitting in the back seat, as dour-looking as ever. Was he hatching a plan to get even with me? Would he cause a disturbance that would make it clear to the inspector that discipline had broken down? Or would he counsel the other boys to give wrong answers to the questions put to them?

'I want to run the Middle Group through the Geography of Ireland', said the inspector.

I felt a lump in my throat. Geography was my weakest subject. And Michael O'Donnell was in Middle Group.

With a heavy heart I lowered the map of Ireland and the examination began. The first question asked was about the linen industry in the North. What was linen made of? Flax.

What did Michael O'Donnell do at this point? He stepped into the breach like a man and brought the rest of the class along with him. He had learned all about flax when he was hired with the big farmers of the Lagan. He had seen fields of it in blue blossom in the early summer. He had worked at the harvesting of it. He had helped to steep it, left it again, and spread it out to dry. He had loaded it and sent it in bales to the local scutching mills. And an old man had explained to him all about the spinning and the weaving of it in the big mills in Belfast. Michael O'Donnell had all this knowledge and he had imparted a lot of it to the rest of the children. For anything that their hero told them they were sure to remember.

The inspector was very pleased.

'That is what I call teaching Geography', he said. 'They are very good. And that big, red-haired lad there is wonderful. I've never met the like of him for complete and accurate answering'.

The inspector left. The day wore on. Michael O'Donnell was giving no trouble. And I was in the throes of remorse for having beaten him in the morning.

When three o'clock came I dismissed the school. Before doing so I whispered to Michael O'Donnell. 'I want you to remain in for a few minutes after the others leave'.

When the rest of the children had gone I called to him. 'Come up here, please'.

He came up.

'You may sit down on that seat'.

He sat down. I began to question him about his smoking habit. His eyes became hard again. His expression became defiant.

'When did you start smoking?' I asked him.

'About two years ago'.

'What kind of tobacco do you smoke?'

'It's turf-mould I smoke most of the time'.

'Do you ever smoke tobacco?'

'When I can get it'.

'It doesn't sicken you?'

'Not now. It used to in the beginning'.

'You did great work today', I said.

He made no reply.

'Here, fill your pipe', said I, handing him my tobacco pouch.

He looked surprised.

'I mean it, Michael', said I. 'Fill your pipe and we'll have a smoke and a chat together'.

He filled the pipe and lit it. It went out, as if he could not control his breathing.

'Light it again', said I. 'Now pull at it slow and steady till you get it going well ... Like that ... You did great work today, Michael. And, God knows, I did not deserve it'.

He made no reply. I saw the corners of his mouth twitching.

'I am sorry I beat you, Michael', I said. 'Very sorry. But I'll never again lay a finger on you'.

He burst out crying. 'It was my own fault, master', he sobbed. 'I provoked you. I'm very sorry, sir'.

'Now don't cry', said I, and I stroked his head. 'It was not your fault. It was mine. But I promise you that I will never again lay a finger on you'.

And I kept that promise.

IV

It was late in the night when I stopped thinking about my teaching days and about Michael O'Donnell. I went past my sleep with the result that I slept late the next morning. When I came down I could see nobody. Evidently all the other guests had gone out. This put a new plan in my head. I would stay late in bed every morning. The waitress would bring me up my breakfast. A few bob would arrange matters.

I went into the dining-room and had my breakfast. Then I went across to the bar, sat on a high stool at the counter and ordered a pint. I was the only customer in the house and I was delighted. I could smoke my pipe and sip my pint in peace without being molested by interfering foreigners.

But just as I was congratulating myself on my good fortune, in walks the American, carrying a parcel in his hand.

'So, you're here', he said. 'I've been looking for you all over the place'.

He pulled up a stool and sat beside me. 'I have a bit of American tobacco here for you', said he, putting the parcel down on the counter.

'But', I protested, 'you will need it for yourself since you don't like our Irish tobacco'.

'I have plenty left', said he … 'Nothing like good tobacco … If you let me have your name and address I will send you a bit from time to time'.

What could I do but offer him a drink?

'I'll try a drop of your Irish malt'.

We talked for a few minutes.

'What are you having?' he asked when he had finished his drink.

'Nothing now, thanks', I replied. 'I am sorry, I must go. I have to go to Dunlewy to see an old friend'.

'Where is Dunlewy?'

'Up at the foot of Errigal'.

'What is Errigal, or where is it?'

'A mountain. The conical, blue peak you see away in the distance'.

'Is there a good road leading up to it?'

'Fairly good as roads go in this part of the country'.

'Very good. Take your time. I'll run you up in the car. Sit down and have another drink'.

I was caught. I could do nothing else but sit down. Between the parcel of tobacco and the offer to drive me to Dunlewy I felt that he had put me under an obligation. There was nothing else for it but sit down and try to talk.

'You were late getting up', he remarked.

'I was', I replied. 'What you said yesterday about putting knowledge into a child with a rod stuck in my mind. When I went to bed I began thinking it over. In the end I went past my sleep'.

'You take life seriously', said he. 'Very few men would let a stray remark they heard in conversation keep them awake at night and put them past their sleep'.

'But', said I, 'what you said about corporal punishment in schools reminded me of a boy I beat once. And I could not let it out of my head'.

'So you are a schoolmaster'.

'Not now. I was once. I ... But we won't go into that now. I beat this boy. Beat him with my fist and knocked him down'.

'What had he done?'

'He was smoking in class'.

'Smoking in class! You were a nice schoolmaster to let things go that far. No wonder you were dismissed if that is what happened to you. You must have been far too soft with the rascal from the beginning and he took your measure. At least, that is my reading of the affair'.

It was an opportunity to talk about something that wasn't strange to me. So I told him the whole story. 'He was the strangest boy I ever knew', I said. 'I beat him and knocked him down but it did not take a feather out of him. His eyes were dry and as hard-looking as polished steel. But the moment I offered him tobacco and said I was sorry for having beaten him, he burst into floods of tears'.

'You got a complete victory over the rascal', said the American.

'On the contrary', said I. 'The victory was his. When I saw him stretched out on the floor with a patch of his poor backside showing through the rent in his trousers, when I saw that and the child's little playthings that fell out of his pockets, it nearly killed me with remorse. And to think of the way he stood by me when the examination came on. Even yet it tears my heart with remorse when I think of it'.

The American caught my hand and clasped it tightly. 'Most people would say you were a fool and still are', said he. 'But you have a tender heart ... A fool, a nation of fools', he went on, as if talking to himself. 'That is what we Americans think about you. We are a progressive, efficient people. At the moment we are the most powerful nation in the world ... But, listening to your story, the thought flashed across my mind that we Americans are too devoted to material progress. Are we going too far with our worship of the almighty dollar? Is there after all something in this little island that we fail to understand? Something that is not altogether foolish? ... By the way, did your boy, what did you call him, Michael O'Donnell, did he show any gratitude to you when he grew up?'

'He could not', I replied. 'We haven't met since he grew up. The following year I left that school, left the profession, as a matter of fact. Years afterwards when I next visited the district I enquired of course for Michael O'Donnell. I was told that he had gone to Scotland and, later on, from there to Canada. I don't know where he is now or if he is alive at all'.

'I would like to have that story published - with your permission, of course. I believe it can be easily arranged. My brother-in-law is on the staff of the *Post*. Hand me down that bottle of liqueur and three glasses', said he to the barman.

'This drink is on me', said I, wondering why he had ordered a third glass.

'On me, this time, please', said he. 'That story of yours is worth a drink any day. And won't the missus enjoy it. I am going to call her in. She will be delighted. I hope you don't mind telling the story a second time. I want her to hear it from yourself. You can make it live. Listening to you telling it, I imagined I could see the whole thing'.

He came down off his stool, went to the door and opened it. His wife was sitting on a seat opposite the bar, reading a book or magazine.

'Come this way, Fanny', he called to her. 'Come right in', said he, holding the door wide open. The wife came in.

'Take a good look at him now, Fanny', said the American. 'That's the guy that floored me with a John L. swipe long ago in the old school in Lettercagh'.

Note

1 This is an English version of Máire's story 'Mé Féin is Fear Mheiriceá' which is published in *Fallaing Shíoda* (An Gúm, 1956), 72-82.

KINGS AND CROWNS[1]

One fine summer day two elderly men - Johnny Neddy and Donal Hughdie Vickey - were sitting on the rocks of the shore smoking their pipes and watching a curragh that was coming in towards them.

'That's young Willie Sweeney', said Johnny Neddy. 'Watch him. He is not quite thirteen years and he has a champion's stroke already. Just watch how he switches the paddle from right to left-hand stroke and how he hooks it into the crest of the wave and pulls the curragh up and right over it. When he grows up he'll be the best curraghman from Malin to Glen Head. Twelve years next August Inishbofin lowered our colours. That was a sad day for the Rosses. But we have a man coming up who will recover our lost crown. O, God, let me live to see the day!'

'I don't think the lad will be a curraghman at all', said Donal Hughdie Vickey. 'He'll be a boxer; that's what he'll be. It's Barney Kilday was telling me. As we all know, Barney has a good pair of hands and he learned boxing when he was in the marines. One day lately he was teaching some of the young lads a bit of sparring down on the strand. 'I sparred with Willie Sweeney for ten minutes and never got one on him', said he to me afterwards. 'Great footwork entirely. A second Jim Corbett'. Them's Barney's very words to me'.

'And what good will fighting be to him, or to us?' asked Johnny Neddy.

'You are thinking only of the name and honour of the Rosses', replied Donal. 'I am thinking of the name and honour of the County of Donegal. When that lad grows up, he'll beat every navvy from the one end of Scotland to the other. It is now thirteen years since the Slogger McCoy from Tyrone beat Carroty Dan. Dan was the last of our great fighters. I was in Westloch that day and it was the saddest day in all my life. Dan fought until his face was battered to pulp. But he had to give in at last. I'll never forget him. When the fight was over he staggered out of the hut. He wouldn't wait until we'd wash the blood off him ... The Slogger still holds the sway and we haven't a man to put against him. That's why I am waiting and hoping and praying for the day when young Willie Sweeney from the Rosses of Donegal will meet him and make him hand over the belt'.

Willie Sweeney grew up to early manhood but he did not want to fill either of the roles that had been planned for him. He would neither fight nor engage in a curragh contest. He had disappointed every man in the parish, except his father. There were two lost crowns and the young man was firmly determined that he would not make the slightest attempt to recover either of them.

'There is a drop of the coward's blood in him', said Donal Hughdie Vickey.

'From his mother's people he got it', said Johnny Neddy.

II

At the age of nineteen Willie Sweeney went across to Scotland to look for work. His father was ill that summer and had to stay at home. So Willie had to go off on his own.

'Now, son', said the father when Willie was leaving, 'stick to Shamey More Khet Neill. Shamey knows a good few farmers around Biggar and he'll do his best to get work for you. If that fails, you could go in by the Lowdens. If you go as far as Linlithgow, try Manorston. I worked there for seven seasons. Tell him who you are and he'll give you a start if he can at all. But, whatever you do, don't go navvying. If you can't get work with the farmers, come back home. No man ever saved a penny at navvy work. And, worse than that, the life grips you and you can't tear yourself away from it. That is why so many fine Rosses men died in the poorhouse in Scotland. They went navvying at your age and the life gripped them'.

Willie Sweeney went across to Scotland. He stuck to Shamey More as his father had advised him. Shamey failed to get work for him. And Willie, still following his father's advice, set out for the Lowdens. When he came as far as the village of West Linton, he met four men who were coming in the opposite direction. Three of them were from Willie's own home townland. The fourth was a stranger - an oldish man with grey hair.

'Where are you heading for?' one of them asked Willie.

'For the Lowdens'.

'You may turn back. We have spent a whole week looking for work in the Lowdens. Not a turn to be got anywhere. The fields are red. The wet spring kept the sowing late. Then the drouth in May burned up everything. The turnips are coming so slow that they are keeping them thinned themselves … We are going over Biggar way to see if we can get a start on the Broughton pipe-track'.

'I passed that way this morning', said Willie, 'but I didn't look for work. I didn't want to. My father advised me to come back home rather than go navvying'.

'And your father was right', said the old man. 'If I had my life to live over again, I'd never do a day's navvying. The navvy's life is a hard one. You can take that from me'.

'I wouldn't be a bit afraid of the work', said Willie, feeling slightly nettled for he was only a very young man. And very young men are sensitive to the slightest implication that they are not fully grown-up.

'I know you would be fit for the work', said the old man. 'Why wouldn't you? But the work is only the softest part of the navvy's life. Wait till the fighting would start'.

'I'll turn back with you', said Willie on the impulse. Then he tried to justify his decision. 'I don't want to go back home without at least earning my passage money. As for fighting, I won't let that bother me. It takes two to make a row and I'll fight with no man'.

'That would be all right if you were left alone'.

'I don't believe the navvies are that bad. I don't believe that any man will walk up to me and hit me without any reason in the world'.

'It happened before', said the old man.

Willie Sweeney turned back with the men. They came to Broughton and got work. And they got lodgings together, in Joe Munday's hut.

Saturday night came but there was no fighting. Willie Sweeney got into conversation with the old man.

'Any harm in asking you what part of Ireland you come from?' said Willie.

'Devil a bit', replied the old man. 'I come from a place called the Rosses in Donegal. Dan O'Donnell is my name. Donal Hughdie Wore they called me at home long ago. In this country I am called Carroty Dan'.

'I am a Rosses man myself', said Willie. 'I've often heard tell of you ... There is no fighting here tonight'.

'By God there isn't for the simple reason that there's no fight left in us', said Dan. 'But if you were in a navvies' hut of a Saturday night twenty years ago, if you saw the men that I knew - Mick Diffy and his brother Ginger, Flanger Campbell and Black Jimmy Boyle. And Carroty Dan although it's himself that says it. But the years have conquered us. And no man from the ould country to take our place. Not one of them would dare to raise his voice above a whisper when Slogger McCoy is about'.

'Who is he?' asked Willie.

'A man from Strabane', replied Carroty Dan. 'He is getting on in years. But, if he is itself, he is still a powerful man. He has a head like a cannon-ball: nothing lighter than a sledgehammer could hurt him. His ribs are steel hoops and his knuckles like the teeth of a harrow ... Bedamn but it is very sad to think that he has all the men of our county cowed. But it can't be helped'.

A few weeks afterwards the news came to Broughton that the Slogger had been seen in Lanark.

'He is on his way here', said Carroty Dan.

'I'd like to see him', said Willie Sweeney.

'If you take my advice, you will clear out before he comes'.

'Why should I do that?'

'If you are here when he comes, he will put fight on you'.

'Why should he put fight on a man he never saw before?'

'Maybe you don't know it yourself', said Dan, 'but you have the cut and build of a fighting man. That's enough for Slogger McCoy. As sure as he sees you, he'll put fight on you. He couldn't sleep at night if he didn't'.

'That is all he will have for it', said Willie. 'I won't fight with him. I don't want to fight with any man. I've come to Scotland to earn my living, not to fight. Another thing, I am staying here only until the harvest is ripe. This is my first time navvying and it will be my last. But I am not going to run away just now and no-one chasing me'.

'Very good. Have it your own way', said the old man.

III

For the next few days Willie Sweeney was thinking over what Carroty Dan had said. 'I won't fight with Slogger McCoy', said he to himself … 'But if he comes up to me and hits me a clout on the face? … No, he won't do that. I can't believe he will. How can he when I tell him I don't want to fight?'

A week passed and the Slogger did not come. A second and a third week passed and no sign of him. The cornfields were turning yellow. Before many days it would be easy to get harvesting work up Kelso way.

Willie Sweeney began his last week's work on the Broughton waterworks. He had planned to leave the following Sunday.

Five days of the week passed. The sixth morning came - Saturday morning. Willie went out to work. It was his last half-day … He worked until the whistle blew at one o'clock. Then he threw down his pick. He was finished forever with navvy work. The next day he would write home to his parents and send them some little money. He would promise them on his word of honour never again to sleep a night in a navvies' hut.

Saturday evening. The men were in good cheer. Some were playing cards at a rickety old table in a corner of the hut. Some were lying on their straw pallets smoking their pipes. Later on they would have a few drinks in the canteen. And then they were looking forward to Sunday's rest.

Willie Sweeney and two others were at the hot plate, each cooking a meal for himself.

Suddenly the conversation stopped. Willie looked back over his shoulder. A strange man was coming across the floor. He was a big, strong-looking man, with thick neck and broad chest and shoulders. And his hair was streaked with grey under the rim of an old, dirty cap. He looked round the hut. There was a savage gleam in his eye. One or two of the men greeted him timidly. His only reply was a growl - like the growl of a vicious dog.

He put down a parcel on one of the old tables. Then he unhooked a black billy-can from his belt, filled it with water and went up to the hot plate.

He made his way in between Willie Sweeney and the man next to him. They stepped aside and made room for the stranger. The stranger was not satisfied with all the room he had been left - although he had more than he needed. He edged up to Willie Sweeney and pushed him rudely with his shoulder. There was no need to tell Willie that he was face to face with the Slogger McCoy.

Willie took his pan off the hot plate and moved away. He went to a corner of the hut and sat down. He was watching the Slogger out of the corner of his eye. 'He is a powerful man even though he is a bit slow in his movements', said he to himself. 'He thought he could provoke me to fight with him. But he failed. And he will fail every time he tries it. I will put in this night without fighting, no matter how many times I am challenged. This is my last night in a navvies' hut. My last night forever'.

The Slogger fried a pound of steak for himself. He made the tea. He took a loaf and cut it into thick slices. Then he sat down and began to eat ravenously.

When he had finished eating, he wiped his mouth on the sleeve of his coat. Then he looked round the hut.

'Any beer in this shack?' he asked.

He was told there was none.

'Never saw you better', said the Slogger, and he went to the corner where Willie Sweeney sat. He put a hand on Willie's shoulder.

'You have the cut and build of a fighting man', said he. 'One has only to look at you to know. But I reckon you haven't yet had your baptism. What about a bit of a spar with Slogger McCoy?'

'I don't want to fight with you', replied Willie. 'I don't want to fight with any man'.

'I don't say you do. But you must fight with me or give in to me'.

'I give in to you'.

'And pay for the drinks?'

'Yes, pay for the drinks. The moment the canteen opens'.

'You are only a coward'.

'You can call me what you like'.

'Well', said the Slogger, 'I've had a good tuck-in and I feel fit for anything. In toppin' fettle for a fight. Not that I need a tuck-in to take on anything in this shack. If I were eating nothing but straw, I'd beat three Donegal men together. I sent the best of them sprawling and it didn't take me long. Carroty Dan, Mick Diffy and his brother

Ginger, Flanger Campbell, Black Jimmy Boyle and the rest of them. I have beaten them all. And with all their pride and boasting they haven't a man to put against me'.

While the Slogger was speaking, Willie Sweeney was looking across at Carroty Dan.

'No', continued the Slogger, 'you have no man now to put in the field. This young man here, big and strong-looking as he is, won't even risk getting a scratch on his lovely face'.

Willie Sweeney got to his feet.

'All right, Slogger', said he. 'I'll fight you as long as I last. That is all any man can do'.

Everyone was amazed at the sudden change in Willie. The Slogger himself wondered at it.

The hut was cleared for action. Chairs and tables were moved into corners. The two combatants stepped out to the middle of the floor and the fight was on.

The Slogger hit out with his powerful right. If only one blow of his had landed where it was aimed, the fight was over. But Willie side-stepped. He did the same again and again. For seven or eight minutes he kept dodging and ducking. The Slogger was getting tired. He was losing his temper.

'Damn you, fight!' he shouted savagely to his opponent. 'Fight and stop dancing around like a circus girl!'

But Willie continued his tactics till he saw his chance. Then, with the full force of his fist and the full drive of his body behind it, he let his opponent have it in the pit of the stomach. The Slogger went down like a log and lay there on the floor as if he were in a swoon.

After a minute or two, he opened his eyes and looked up at his conqueror.

'I am beaten', he said, faintly and sadly.

Willie caught him by the hand and helped him to his feet. The Slogger sat in a corner for a while, his face buried in his hands. He seemed stunned, as if he could hardly realise what had happened. At last, he got up slowly, picked up his little belongings and proceeded to walk towards the door.

'Where are you going?' asked Carroty Dan.

The Slogger turned round and faced Dan.

'Where am I going?' said he. 'Somewhere, anywhere, but I can't stay here. I must go away'.

'Why must you go away?' said Dan. 'Stay where you are, at least until Monday morning. We'll send down to the canteen for a few bottles of beer'.

Willie Sweeney and the others begged him to stay. But it was no use. He thanked them.

'Maybe I'd drop in sometime before the winter but I can't stay now'.

'But where will you spend the night?' asked Willie.

'In a haystack. All alone. The way I want to be'.

'In heaven's name, Slogger, have a bit of sense!' implored Carroty Dan. 'Stay the night with us at least'.

'Dan', replied the Slogger, 'I am very thankful to you. But you didn't stay till morning the night long ago I beat you in Westloch. I wanted you to stay. You wouldn't. It was the depth of winter. You went out into the blizzard. Ginger Diffy didn't stay in Wishaw the night I beat him. Black Jimmy Boyle didn't stay where I had beaten him. Nor Flanger Campbell, nor any of the rest of them. They all went off. They couldn't stay. They would die of a broken heart if they couldn't get away to some lonely place. A king can't stay where he has lost his crown.

Good-bye, all. Good-bye and good luck, young champion', said he, shaking Willie Sweeney's hand.

And he went away.

IV

Sonny Neill and I came to the town of Peebles one afternoon, towards the end of summer. We were tired and downhearted for we had been tramping the roads for over a week and had failed to get work. And the harvest would not be ripe for cutting for at least three weeks to come.

'Where will we go now?' said I.

'We'll go in here to the Cross Keys till we have a pint of beer and rest our bones. And tomorrow, I think in God's name we should head for Lanark. Maybe we'd get a start on the new dam they are building at Cora Linn'.

'I don't like to go navvying', said I.

'Neither do I', said Sonny, 'but what else can we do? In any case, we'll go in here and rest for a while'.

We went into the pub. There was only one other customer in the bar. He was perched on a high stool at the counter with a tankard of beer in front of him. We walked a few steps past him and sat down. I could not keep my eyes off the big man on the stool. He was coming on to middle-age and he was a man of powerful size and build. His hair was almost white and his face was a network of scars. Sonny and I began talking about our chances of work on the dam at Cora Linn on the Clyde.

'It will take us the best part of two days to make the journey', said I. 'And it is only a chance we get work when we arrive. If we could meet anyone who was round that way lately, someone who might be able to tell us what our chances are'.

'Where were you thinking of going, lads?' asked the big man, turning round to face us.

'To Cora Linn on the Clyde', replied Sonny.

'To the dam', said the big man. 'Easy enough to get a start there now. They are looking for more men'.

'Were you round that way lately?'

'I was'.

'Pull up your stool and tell us all about it'.

He came up and sat beside us. 'I worked there until the beginning of May', he began. 'Not a bad place at all'.

'Drink that', said Sonny, and he made a sign to the barman to fill the tankard again.

'Five pence an hour they pay on the dam', continued the big man. 'Good accommodation. A fine, large hut, with two new, hot plates. You will be all right there till the harvest is ready. For the whole season if you care to stay ... But', said he after a pause, 'it is strange that neither of you have asked me why I left it and went on the tramp'.

'That is your own affair', said Sonny.

'I suppose it is', he said. 'Still, it does a man good at times to talk to others about his own affairs. It takes some of the load off the mind. But perhaps I ought to tell you who I am. Have you ever heard tell of Willie Sweeney from the Rosses of Donegal once upon a time?'

Had we ever heard of Willie Sweeney? Had we heard of Cúchulainn and Colmcille and the rest of Ireland's ancient heroes and saints?

Each of us shook his hand.

'Sure your name is a household word at home', said I.

'Where do you come from?' he asked.

'From the Rosses', replied Sonny. 'I am a son of Niall Himisheen. This lad is a son of Felimy Roe'.

'You are both related to me, on my mother's side', said Willie. 'The O'Donnells of Purt'.

'My father was in the hut in Broughton the day long ago you beat Slugger McCoy', said Sonny.

Willie lapsed into silence. After a rather long pause, he spoke again.

'Many a time', said he, 'I said that I could not have avoided that fight - that it was forced on me. Still, if I didn't want to fight, no one could have forced me. And I would have let the Slogger go his way and let someone else put manners on him. Of course I got great provocation. He shouldered me away from the hot plate. He heaped insults on me. I gave in to him. Then he said that if he had nothing to eat but straw he would beat three Donegal men together. He called me a coward. I took it all. I had my mind made up not to fight except in self defence. And I was almost certain he would not attack me. But, as if the devil were guiding me, I looked across at Carroty Dan. And there he was with agony in every inch of his face. I'll never forget the look he gave me. Not egging me on to fight. No, not that, but blaming me for not having left, as he had advised me, before the Slogger came and disgraced the old county once again. It was that agonising look on Carroty Dan's face that made me take on the Slogger'.

'He was no match for you, I heard my father say', said Sonny.

'It wasn't I beat him but the years', said Willie. 'He was coming on to middle-age at the time and, of course, getting stiff and slow in his movements. I was young and supple. But he was a clean fighter, I'll say that for him. And he was dangerous to the end. He had a right would knock down a Clydesdale. But I kept him running round after me until I tired him and broke his temper. At last, I saw my chance and landed one on him that finished the battle'.

'So there you are', he resumed after a pause. 'At times it takes only the merest trifle to put a man on the road he is to travel for the rest of his life. The day I met Slogger McCoy I had my mind firmly made up to leave for the early harvest the next morning. I would never again do a day's navvying. I would work with the farmers until the beginning of winter and then go home. I would do that every year. In due course I would get married. I would have a little place of my own in the Rosses to end my days in'.

He became silent and sad-looking.

'How long is it since you were home in Ireland?' I asked, feeling I had to say something.

'Twenty-four years', he replied. 'Exactly twenty-four years since I fought the Slogger McCoy in Broughton. I didn't go to the harvest that year nor since. I was a king that day in Broughton. And a king doesn't like to throw away his crown the day it's put on his head. But it would be easy to make me go home now if I had any home to go to. I am no longer a king. I've lost my crown. Lost it last Saturday in the Cora Linn. That is why I am here today'.

'Maybe you were drunk', said Sonny, trying to console him.

'Not one drop of drink had I taken', said Willie. 'I just wasn't a man for him. I was beaten in a clean, fair and square fight'.

'Who is he or where is he from?' asked one of us.

'From the Rosses', replied Willie Sweeney. 'A son of Black Murty Gallagher from Tubberkeen. Twenty years of age, he is. Last year was his first year in this country. I had nothing against him, nor he had nothing against me. But the moment he came into the hut and saw me, he put fight on me. I would either have to fight him or surrender. I wouldn't surrender, of course. So the two of us stripped and the fight was on. Three times I floored him. But it was no use. He was no sooner down than he was up again. At last he gave me one and, for a while, I didn't know that I had ever been alive. When I came to, he was kneeling beside me with his finger on my wrist to see if the life was in me'.

'That's why I left Cora Linn on Saturday evening. I walked all night. Young Gallagher, the man that beat me, begged me to stay. So did the others. But I couldn't. I wanted to get out into the darkness and the loneliness. No king wants to stay where he has lost his crown'.

Note

1   This is an English version of the story 'Dómhnall Ó Baoighill' which is published in *An Bhratach* (An Gúm, 1959) 48-60.

LOVE AND WAR[1]

Donal More McGilligan was the biggest and strongest man in the Rosses in his day. Along with being big and strong, he was fearless. His exploits on sea were as remarkable as his ingenuity for baffling the police when he was making poteen.

His wife was proud of him. She was convinced that no man was a match for him, that he could go places in his curragh in stormy weather where no enemy dared to pursue him. His old mother lived with them. She was proud of her son but she knew he was not invincible, particularly when he was up against the law and its agents. She often said so to him: 'You are big and strong and fearless, son. No man in the Rosses would dare to meet you in a fight. But Cúchulainn was stronger than you, yet he was conquered. What the men of Ireland with their spears and swords failed to do, the little, humpy sons of Cailitín[2] did with their magic spells'.

'But, mother, there is nobody here now to put a magic spell on me, on myself or on anyone else'.

'It is the same as a magic spell son. The power of gold can bring down any man. For one thing, there is the informer. You don't know who he is. He may be your neighbour, your kinsman for that matter. He passes for an honest man. He wouldn't steal a farthing in a thousand years. Yet he won't hesitate to give information to the police for money. A few months ago you did a brave thing and a clever thing. You went to Inishfree to make poteen a few hours before the storm broke. You knew it was coming. You had a supply of food. The police knew you were on the island and knew what you were doing there. They could see the smoke of your fire from Inishinny, but they couldn't go in; the raging sea was between them and you. That didn't worry them much; they'd get you coming out. You tricked them again. When you had finished and when the storm was dying down a bit, you took your stuff to another island and hid it there. The next day was calm; you set out for home. The police were down there on the shore waiting for you. You sailed up and landed under their nose and not even a smell of poteen off you. It was very clever. But don't try the same trick again. Remember that the sons of Cailitín got Cúchulainn. What I mean is this: remember that the informer is somewhere, and that he is expecting a nice penny for giving information that will get you caught'.

II

There was of course a bailiff in the Rosses at the time. He had a squint in one of his eyes, and for that reason he was never called any other name but Squinty. He was one of the most hated men in the country. On two occasions he got a sound beating when trying to make a seizure. Ever afterwards he never came to the scene of operation without a guard of police.

In the course of time he took on an extra duty to perform. For years Jack Phaddy Wore from Kildoney had the job of guarding the Yellow River against poachers. For seven years Jack filled the post without once having a case in the Cloghanlee law court. Jack had a formula for squaring matters with his conscience. 'Don't let me catch you poaching', he would say. Which was understood –

and rightly so – to mean, 'Wait till you get me at one end of the river before you begin to poach at the other end'.

At last Jack was suspected of conniving at, if not actually encouraging poaching, and he was relieved of his post.

Squinty took over.

Early one morning, after the October floods had begun, Donal More McGilligan went out and speared a fine salmon. He wasn't a bit afraid of being caught. It was early at the time. Donal was certain that Squinty could not be within miles of him at the time. He was walking along the edge of the river when he heard a cry from the opposite bank. It was Squinty. 'I have you, Donal More McGilligan', said he.

'Go home and forget about it', said Donal.

'I suppose I will forget about it when it is all over. But not till then'.

'Listen', said Donal, 'if you breathe a word of this to a living soul, I'll break every bone in your body. I mean what I say. Every bone in your lousy body'.

'We'll see', said Squinty, moving away. He did not wish to prolong the dialogue. He wanted to get away from what could easily become a dangerous position. He had two cases against his man – the spearing of the salmon and the threat of violence. Donal would get three months for each offence. After six months in Derry jail he would come back a chastened man.

'It's a fine one', said his wife to Donal, when he came in holding the fish by the gills. 'Where did you land him?'

'At the bend below the White Rock'.

'Anyone else out?'

'Only one - Squinty'.

'Squinty! He must have left home long before dawn. Did he see you?'

'I should think he did', replied Donal and he told them of his encounter with the bailiff.

'Squinty won't stop till he gets what's coming to him', said the wife.

'He was damn near getting it just now', replied her husband. 'As near as he ever went to it. He kept on the far side of the river. Even then he wasn't safe. I had to fight down my anger. More than once I was on the point of plunging across the river and giving him a beating he'd remember till his dying day. As it was I frightened him to within an inch of his life. He'll never breathe a word of it to a living soul'.

'Let us hope not', said the wife, beginning to feel somewhat uneasy.

'He won't', repeated Donal. 'I put the fear of God into him'.

'I would not be too sure, son', said the old woman. 'Jack Phaddy Wore was put out of that job because they knew after seven years that Jack would never go into the courthouse in Cloghanlee and swear on the Holy Book against a neighbour. Squinty didn't take the job to follow in Jack's footsteps. Jack Phaddy Wore was a man: Squinty is one of the sons of Cailitín. I am afraid you'll hear more about this, my son'.

Her forecast was only too soon verified.

At this time Donal More McGilligan's eldest son Cathal was a lad of about eleven or twelve years of age. He was a fine strong lad, resembling his father in many ways. He was not in the least perturbed over his grandmother's gloomy forebodings, for he had unbounded faith in his father's strength and valour. No man could get the better of his father. Squinty would never breathe a word about the salmon or about the threat. He would be too much afraid.

But on the afternoon of that same day the poor boy was sadly disillusioned. Three policemen armed with rifles came to the house and ordered Donal More to accompany them to the barracks. The boy could hardly believe his eyes when he saw his father walk out the door as meek as a lamb. He said that later on to Micheal Roe, an old man from the neighbourhood.

'You thought', said the old man, 'your father would take the three of them and knock their heads together and then kick them out the door. That is exactly what he would have done if they hadn't been armed. But you saw the guns they had. Harmless-looking things. But each of them could spit death at you in a second. A dwarf with a loaded gun is more than a match for a giant without one'.

Donal More's trial came on. Squinty swore what he had to swear. The magistrate imposed a sentence of three months for poaching, and a further three months for the threat to the bailiff. He concluded by saying that he was sorry that the law did not allow him to impose a more severe sentence, especially in the case of the threat of violence. Society, he said, would fall to pieces if State servants were thus molested in discharge of their lawful duty.

Donal More McGilligan was sent to Derry jail. After six months he returned home, compelled to admit that he had been totally defeated by Squinty.

Meanwhile Squinty continued his activities. He lived in the townland of Cromuck at the foot of the hills about two miles from the village of Cloghanlee, on the Glenties side. Squinty was quite happy at his work. Whether the neighbours were friendly or not didn't matter to him. But his wife was anything but happy. She was concerned with the fate of their two children, a boy and a girl. What kind of life would these children have in the Rosses when they grew up? Would they be ostracised? Were they more sensitive than their father and would they feel humiliated when they grew up? The mother was continually harping on this string. As they were growing up and becoming more observant the children themselves began to be afraid of the future that was in store for them. The upshot of it all was that each of them at the age of sixteen left the Rosses. They had been placed somewhere but nobody knew their destination. There were guesses and rumours. Some said the boy had crossed to England, some said that the girl was working in a shop in Derry. But all that the people knew for certain was that Squinty's progeny was gone from the Rosses.

III

Cathal McGilligan grew up to manhood. Rapid changes were taking place in Ireland. One Easter Monday morning a small band of men challenged the might of an empire in arms. The insurrection was crushed in a week but a new spirit was making itself felt. There was talk and hope of the Ireland of the future. The yoke of the foreigner would be thrown off. Jobbery and place-hunting would be abolished.

Unlike his father, Cathal McGilligan had been to school. He had learned English. He could read the newspapers. He could get at least the gist of Mitchel's *Jail Journal*. He could read rousing songs and ballads like 'The Men of the West' and 'The Rising of the Moon'. He could read all this in the only tongue through which the gospel of freedom and nationality had come to Ireland since her own powerful and exquisitely beautiful language had received its death-blow on the field of Kinsale.

Cathal had become an ardent nationalist. Hence it is not to be wondered at that he joined the first company of Volunteers that was formed in the Rosses. He continued to practise as much drill and as many exercises as he could for four or five months. But he could not remain at home. He must earn his living. Early in summer he went over to Scotland.

He went to work in Glasgow where, he soon discovered, there were two Volunteer companies, composed of either Irish exiles or the sons of Irish exiles. Cathal joined one of these companies and devoted all the time he could spare to Volunteer work, fully determined to go back to Ireland when the day should come.

And then one day a beautiful, young girl entered into his life. It was at a concert held by one of the Irish clubs. This girl was a beauty if there was ever one. Between her raven black hair and her eyes like diamonds … But why should I try to describe what I cannot describe? She wore an Irish costume and, in addition to her other attractions, she had a beautiful singing voice. Everybody was fascinated with her when she came on to the stage. When she came to her last number Cathal McGilligan was spellbound. Not alone was she a beautiful girl and an exquisite singer but she symbolised the Ireland of his dreams. It could be said of him that 'fancy bore him to the palest star', as he listened to the chorus of her last song:

'All around my hat I'll wear a tricolour ribbon, O,
All around my hat until death comes to me.
And if anyone should ask me why I am wearing it,
It's all for my true love I never more shall see'.

Needless to say Cathal McGilligan made it his business to get to know this beautiful maiden, with whom he was already madly in love. She worked as a waitress in a teashop on the South Side. Her name was Rosaleen Cannon and she came from Donegal - from a place called Glengesh, a few miles outside the town of Ardara. Before long she was as much in love with the young man as he was with her.

One day she told him she intended to go back home for a spell in two or three months' time. She lived with her grandparents and she did not like to leave them by themselves too long. Cathal decided to go home at the same time. He persuaded himself that the time was near at hand when the Rosses Volunteers would justify their existence.

However, he had occasion to go home sooner than he had planned. One day he had a letter from his mother containing sad news. His grandmother was dying and had expressed a wish to see him. He said he would have to go at all costs with which his sweetheart agreed.

They made their plans. Rosaleen was to go home in two months. As soon as she had arrived she would write to him and let him know. He would come to Ardara for a few days. He would, of course, visit her grandparents, and she was certain he would find them friendly.

Cathal came home.

'How is granny?' he asked as he came in the door.

'She is asleep at the moment', replied his mother. 'She mentions your name very often; gives the impression that there is something she wants to say to you before she dies'.

'What happened her?'

'Old age, I suppose. The doctor calls it a clot, whatever that is. He says it can only be a matter of a few days. She was anointed on Monday. I think she'll be happy when she sees you and that she will say what she has to say to you when she gets one of her clear spells. Strange the way it takes her. At times she raves away. At other times she is as sensible as you are now. This morning she wanted to know when you were coming. Tonight, I told her'.

'I want to say something to him', says she. 'I wanted to spare him another cruel blow like the one he got the day long ago his father was arrested'.

'That's strange', said Cathal. 'What can be in her mind at all?'

'But wait till I tell you the next thing she said'.

'Fanny', says she, 'Colmcille came into the room a little while ago. He came up and stood beside the bed', says she, 'and he raised his hand over me in blessing. Then says he to me: 'You'll go straight to heaven when you die. But before you go, tell your grandson that he is not to expect too much for the day could come when some of the leading warriors of the Craobh Rua will go over to the sons of Cailitín and they will divide the spoils between them'.

'What under heaven can she have meant by that?' asked Cathal.

'Of course, she was only raving'.

'I know, but all the same it was a strange thing, a thing that would stick in the mind'.

The following day the old woman had very few lucid intervals. And, during those intervals, she was not inclined to talk. Obviously she was too tired to talk. The next day she passed peacefully away without leaving any message to her grandson except the fantastic imaginings of her delirium.

IV

Cathal joined his old company at home. Things were already becoming lively in the Rosses. The police had left one or two isolated outposts. Two prisoners had been rescued from their R.I.C. escort on their way to Derry jail. The Falmore barracks had been raided successfully.

Cathal McGilligan was glad. He was light-hearted and happy - happy to have won the heart of a beautiful girl, a charming singer whose inspiring songs would be enough to waken Ireland from the slumber of centuries. He was getting a weekly bulletin from her from Glasgow. At last she came home and wrote to him suggesting that he should come to Ardara for a day or two. He was only too glad to get the invitation. He spent three days in the town. Rosaleen would come in to meet him. Then they would walk out to Glengesh and spend the afternoon with the grandparents. They were a very friendly old pair. It was evident that they would be quite pleased to have this fine young man as their grandson-in-law. Then he and his love would have a little home ready-made for them.

But it is impossible to be happy for long in this world. Cathal was in love and was loved in return. But, at times, the thought would occur to him: if I get killed in this struggle? It was an annoying thought. He would banish it from his mind today; it came back tomorrow.

Sometimes he visualised her as she was when he had first seen and heard her ... Would she have to wear that ribbon in reality some day? Would she have to say from the depth of a broken heart:

'It's all for my true love I never more shall see'.

At last, however, something happened that dispelled his dark thoughts and made him feel glad that he was a member of the I.R.A. The whirligig of time had brought its revenge.

The Volunteers in the Rosses came to the conclusion that there was a spy in the parish and their suspicions fell on Squinty. It was easy to suspect him. First of all, there was his horrid past record. Then he must be hard up for money. The courts had ceased to function. There were no more decrees to be executed, no more seizures to be made. It was decided to set a trap for Squinty - to let out a piece of bogus information that no one else could get. A meeting of Volunteer officers to be held in a certain house on a certain date and at a certain hour. The plan worked. A lorry-load of armed police came from Letterkenny and raided the venue specified in the information they got. It was enough to convince the Volunteers that Squinty was an enemy spy.

He was tried in his absence and sentenced to leave the county before a certain date. This was the whirligig of time giving Cathal McGilligan an opportunity he would not miss for the world. He went to the senior officer in the brigade and put his request before him. He wanted to be the man that would serve the deportation order on Squinty.

'But why?' asked the officer.

Cathal told his story.

'Very good', said the officer. 'You will get the order to serve on him and you can add a stern warning from me that it must be complied with before the date specified. But remember this much: no matter what he says to you, no matter how he provokes you (and he has a wicked tongue, I believe), you are not to touch him. You are not to lay a finger on him. If you do, you'll suffer for it. This is not a matter of private revenge. A republic founded on private revenge and personal grievances is not the one we are fighting to establish. We believe Squinty is a spy. We are punishing him for it or rather we are banishing him for the sake of the security of our organization and of our men'.

'But I can say what I like to him?'

'You may, if that does you any good. But, once more I repeat you are not to lay a finger on him … Here is the order. You will go and serve it on him right now'.

Cathal mounted his bicycle and started off from Cromuck where Squinty lived. As he went along he cast his mind back twelve years. The scene in his father's on that day was vividly before his mind. Three policemen armed with rifles taking his father away to the barracks. Then the trial. Squinty in the witness-box telling his story. Then the sentence … A cell in Derry jail.

Cathal was rehearsing in his mind what he would say to the informer: 'You have been convicted as a spy, Squinty, and the I.R.A. are punishing you for your treason. But, in addition to your sentence, I have a few words to say to you on my own behalf. Twelve years ago you were a strong man, a very strong man, because you had British bayonets at your back. The same British bayonets protected you while you carried on your diabolic trade, while you seized the widow's cow and left the poor orphans without a drop of milk. I was only a boy the day long ago you had my father arrested. My heart was sore that day. I was in despair. I thought you and your gang would rule forever. But the wheel has turned. I am here today to serve this order on you - an order to clear out of the county before the date specified - and I can tell you I am glad to have the same mission to fulfil'.

He was very glad as he went along on his journey - almost as glad as if he were on his way to Ardara to meet his love … He must pay her a visit soon. She would be delighted to hear they had caught the informer. He remembered the stirring national songs she used to sing at their Irish gatherings in Glasgow. She had great faith in the future of Ireland. Some women were like that. They did not base their conclusions on reason. They were possessed of a higher power. They knew in their hearts what was right. Such women as Rosaleen could save a nation even if the men did nothing but look on!

He turned in the direction of the little bridge. It was the road that brought him to Squinty's. He could see the house away at the foot of the hill. He saw a woman coming towards him. It could not be … It was … It was Rosaleen all right. This was great. Two sources of gladness in one day. But why didn't she let him know she was coming?

They met on the bridge.

'Rosaleen, darling', said Cathal coming off his bicycle and standing the machine against the wall of the bridge. He took his love in his arms and kissed her tenderly.

'I didn't expect to see you here', he said. 'Why didn't you let me know you were coming?'

'I didn't know myself until last night. The school-teacher and his wife were coming down - she wanted to see some knitwear in the Co-op. factory - and they offered me a lift. I thought I'd like to come, to see what your Rosses was like so I walked out this way to kill time. It is a wild country but beautiful in its own way'.

'It will be bleak-looking before long. The sky is full of snow. When are you going back?'

The girl looked at her wrist-watch. 'In about three quarters of an hour', she replied.

This was disconcerting to Cathal. It was interfering with his planned programme. He could go to Squinty's, serve the order on the delinquent and be back a few minutes before the girl left the village. But he would have no time for saying to Squinty all he wanted to say to him. However, that could not be helped. He would forego the pleasure for the sake of a few minutes with his darling.

'Listen', he said hurriedly, 'I must go out to Cromuck. See the thatched house at the foot of the hill?'

Rosaleen sat on the wall of the bridge.

'I have to serve a deportation order on the man who lives there', continued Cathal. 'He has been convicted as a spy and I have been given the task of serving the order on him. Apart from his treason this time, he has a very black record - the worst in the county. You may have heard of him - even as far away as Glengesh. They call him Squinty'.

The girl buried her face in her hands and set up a heart-rending scream. Her whole body shook with emotion.

'Rosaleen, Rosaleen, what in the name of God is wrong with you?' asked the young man. 'What has happened to you? Tell me, tell me, darling'.

After some time she looked up at him with the most sorrowful and woebegone face that can be imagined.

'O God in heaven', she sobbed. 'My poor father … Banished from his little home … With the snows of winter coming … Hunted like a mad dog … And every door in the country shut against him … O Blessed Mother of God … '

But she could say no more. She broke down again and continued to cry bitterly.

Notes

1 This is an English version of the story 'Éiric' which is published in *Cúl le Muir agus Scéalta Eile* (An Gúm, 1961) 74-91.
2 He was the chief druid of Medb and Ailill. The Ulster Cycle of Gaelic literature is referred to here.

MY NUT-BROWN MAID[1]

Manus Brocach was an old man when I first saw him. He had spent fifty years in foreign lands. At the age of twenty he left his native home – a heather glen in the Rosses – and he was seventy when he returned. He came back when he was no longer able to work. The walls of the old cabin where he had been born and brought up were still standing. He had a roof of sorts put on it, and he settled down to live as best he could on his old age pension.

He was odd in ways. We – that is, the young people – thought he was born that way. But the few surviving old people who had known him in his young days remembered him when he was full of life and gladness and joy. 'A grand young man he was', they would say. 'Sure we remember him when he was the darling of the parish. And the way he could compose a song or a story – just while he would be walking from the top to the bottom of the Glen. What came over him at all? Maybe it's too proud he was. God save everybody from the sin of pride. Wasn't it the beginning of all evil?'

In the course of time we got the first explanation of what had happened him. A Spaniard had stabbed him in the head one night he was in a row in a seaport town. (The Spaniards were very vicious, they said). Ever since they said Manus was not like another body. This was a likely enough explanation for the old man had a scar about three inches long across the left temple. The mark was there and no mistake about it. Sure enough, they said, that was the blow that put him off the balance.

Never again would he laugh the old, hearty laugh. Never again would he compose a song or a story!

But, in every community, there are people who refuse to believe the first story, no matter how plausible it may be. There were a few such people in the Glen. They pretended to have dug deep down to the root of things and to have discovered the real cause of the change that had come over old Manus. 'A blow on the head', said Mary Feggy Tammy one evening in our house. 'That's all moonshine. We know where he got the blow. I know it all. I have the whole story from a man who knew him for years in America'.

According to Mary, the real cause of Manus' 'little madness' had been a love affair. It had been caused by a blow on the heart, not on the head. And the weapon was wielded, not by a drunken sailor, but by a fair female. Poor Manus! It was the old story, in all its details. A beautiful damsel entered into his life when he was in the prime and flower of his manhood. He fell in love with her, at first sight. And she? Well, she was as false as she was fair. She encouraged and flattered him until he thought he was lord and master of her heart. Then one fine day he proposed to her. She looked at him in surprise. Surprised that he should be guilty of such foolish presumption. And she set him off about his business. They parted. He saw her no more. A few months afterwards she married another man. And poor Manus' dream was shattered to bits. 'Ever since he is a bit astray in the head', concluded Mary Feggy Tammy.

I was glad when I heard Mary's version of the story. I preferred it to the first tale for more reasons than one. In the first place, it made my old man a hero in my eyes. He was no longer a drunken rowdy; he was the victim of a noble passion. In the second place I was in love at the time, with a beautiful nut-brown maiden from Portnamoe. And I was convinced that it was my gift of story-telling that first attracted me to her. Manus Brocach's story would be a great one if only I could get it in full detail from himself. Here was real tragedy, the stuff that great stories are made of. I could imagine my nut-brown maiden enthralled listening to it, as Desdemona once listened to Othello.

How could I get the old man to open his heart to me? He was sour and sullen. He had no time for the young generation. If one of us bade him the time of day he would hardly answer. There was not much chance that he would lay bare the secrets of his heart to a *smugachán* of twenty years.

II

At last I hit on a plan. I got a half-pint of poteen and a bar of tobacco, and one evening I set out for the Glen. When I came to the top of Ardbane I stood and looked across the bay. There is where my nut-brown maiden lives, I thought to myself. In that long white-washed thatched house in the lip of the sea. If I am successful in this mission that I am on I'll have a great story to tell her when I meet her next Sunday evening.

I felt very happy and I began to sing an old Rosses song that was a favourite with me at the time bcause it was so fitting for the occasion.

> 'She was fair and she was charming
> Pure as the lily in yonder glade;
> Her eye did glint like the star of morning;
> She was a beauty was my nut-brown maid'.

I found old Manus in his little cabin, sitting on a low stool and looking into the embers of a dying fire. He turned round on the stool when he heard my footsteps. I spoke to him as cheerfully as I could. He merely growled in reply. I spoke a second time. Another growl. I did not know what to say. I was afraid of this old man.

At last I fumbled for the bottle and I handed it to him.

'Take a sup of this', said I, 'and tell me what you think of it. I believe it is good'.

'Who are you?' he asked me, taking the bottle from my hand.

I told him.

'Take a seat if you can find one', said he. 'I knew your grandfather well … Of course, I never saw you before. How could I?'

'You will have a drink from me even though you don't know me', said I.

He did not take much pressing. He put the bottle to his mouth and drank a long draught. Then he put it down on the hearth-stone beside him and he took an old clay pipe from the hob. He tried to light it but there was nothing in it but ashes.

'What about filling it?' said I, and I handed him the plug of tobacco.

'You are a good lad', said he, and he began cutting the tobacco with a rusty, old knife.

He filled the pipe and lit it. He smoked in silence for about ten minutes. By the end of that time we could hardly see each other's faces through the clouds of smoke.

By degrees the old man found his speech. 'I didn't expect', said he, 'that any of the young people would visit me or be so kind to me'.

'What made you think that?' I asked. 'I would have visited you long ago, but – '.

'Say it out', he snapped. 'But you were afraid. You had heard things about me. You had been told that I was an odd creature and that I wanted nobody near me ... Of course I am odd. I know it. But maybe there is a good reason for it'.

Of course there was a good reason for it. I knew there was. And I was glad when I saw that he was about to plunge straight into the heart of the story without any preliminaries. But I was taken aback by his next sentence: 'Anyone coming back to the Glen after fifty years' absence couldn't be anything else but odd', said he. 'You are odd if you say that people should listen to one another in their turn and not all talk together. You are odd if you are not like your neighbours. That means you are not like another body. That in turn means that you are crazy. Crazy! That is what they say I am. If your grandfather were alive he would not say I was crazy'.

He took another drink out of the bottle. Then he began to relate some of his adventures at sea. This, of course, was not the story I was after. But that would come later on, I hoped. I thought it better not to interrupt him. At least not until I found a good opening.

He was a marvellous story-teller. Something altogether different from any that I had heard before. 'I remember one night off the coast of Africa', he began. 'We expected to sight land by sunrise on the next day. Suddenly the order was given to furl the sails. We had just stripped her when the squall struck. We had to run before it for five long hours. It was a terrifying night. You would think the dome of heaven had been torn into rags and the rags were being blown across the face of the moon. I can see that ship yet, poised on the top of a huge mountain of water. I can hear her timbers creaking and groaning as she fell heavily into the trough of the sea. I can hear her sighing as if she were afraid she would never come up again'.

When he had exhausted his store of credible, though unlikely, stories he launched out into fairy-tales. Here again his narrative was so vivid that I was almost forced to believe him. He had seen the three rocks known as The Stags set out under full sail one morning to invade and reconquer Tory. They skimmed over the surface of the water like seagulls until they reached a point off the foreland. Then they were seen by the Tory folk; and of course the spell was broken. The Stags had to turn back to where they had left. They would try again and again, he said. They would keep on trying to the end of time but they would never reach Tory. The Stags were pagan druids that Colmcille had turned into rocks. Every seventh year they would attempt, on May morning, to come back and reconquer the island from which they had been banished. But they would never succeed: Colmcille had seen to that!

Another morning at dawn, he said, he saw a fairy palace on the outermost tip of the Grey Headland. He was one of a boat's crew on their way back from the fishing-ground. 'It was a marvellous sight that same palace', said he. 'We could see its white pinnacles towering over the cliffs. When we were within a few hundred yards of it every one of us looked away from it. Seems we had to. When we looked shorewards again there was no palace. Nothing but the bare, bleak headland and the sea shivering in the dawn'.

He took another drink.

'Like something one would dream about. The Kingdom of heaven', said I, anxious to say something.

'Yes, dream perhaps', said the old man. 'But only dream. The fairy palace that I've been telling you about, beautiful though it was, was no more like the Kingdom of heaven than this poor, little hut is like the king of Spain's castle. I saw heaven, boy, so I know what I am talking about'.

'You saw heaven? In your dreams?'

'No, it was no dream. I was as wide awake as I am now. Have you never heard the old people talk how I was missing for nine days long ago when I was about your age now? Looking at heaven I was all the time. It was thought, of course, that I was drowned. They searched every creek and cave along the whole coast of the Rosses looking for my body. At last they concluded that I had been swept out by the ebb-tide, away beyond Aran and they gave up the search. My father and mother were heart-broken'.

I had not heard a word of this fantastic tale but I pretended to some recollection of it. I wanted to humour him. I would listen to everything he had to say in the hope that in the end he would come to the story I was after – the story of the woman who broke his heart. I wanted to have it for my nut-brown maiden in Portnamoe. It would make a far greater appeal to her than a ship in a storm or fantastic yarns about a vision of the Kingdom of heaven.

'It is true', he continued, 'every word of it. One fine morning I was lying on the broad of my back in a hollow between two sand-dunes. I heard the warbling of a bird in the sky over me. I looked up and I saw a tiny speck of light like a star. It spread quickly until it covered the whole sky. It was then I saw the Kingdom of heaven'.

'What was it like?' I asked.

'Couldn't describe it', he replied. 'As Mongan said to Colmcille: 'If I had a thousand heads and a thousand tongues in each head, and if I were to live to the end of time, I could not describe the least of heaven's glories … ' The vision lasted, I thought, two or three minutes. Then darkness came. I felt very cold and very hungry. I got up and made for home … The sun was just rising over the peak of Errigal. Then I realised the vision had lasted a whole day and night … When at last I came home, I found my father and mother sitting in gloomy silence over a dying fire. As I crossed the floor, I saw horror in their eyes. They thought I had come back from the dead … Bit by bit I was told the whole story. I had been missing for nine days. Imagine that! Nine whole days and nights! And I thought the vision lasted only two or three minutes'.

III

He filled his pipe again. Then he handed me back the remainder of the tobacco. 'Keep it', I said. 'I don't smoke. I got it specially for yourself'.

'You are a good youngster', said he. 'A very good youngster. And, in a way, I don't deserve your kindness'.

'Why do you say that?'

'Because what I've been telling you is just a bundle of lies. Not one word of truth in it'.

'It doesn't matter. I could sit here and listen to you for a whole week. I thought I had heard the best story-tellers in the Rosses. I have heard so-and-so and so-and-so. But you are miles ahead of them all'.

'They weren't story-tellers', said the old man. 'They were only what we called *seanchaí*s. They could recite tales of the Red Branch and of the Fianna. Accurately enough, I admit, but I would not call them story-tellers for that. The story-teller must have the gift of imagination'.

'Which means he must be a poet', I ventured.

'Exactly', replied the old man. 'No man can be a real story-teller unless he has the gift of poetry'.

It was getting late. The darkness was gathering around us, inside and outside the old cabin. Would I ever get him to tell the story of the woman who broke his heart – the woman for the sake of whose memory he had lived a life of loneliness? I was anxious to have this story to relate it to my nut-brown maiden. I would keep at him at least for another half-hour. 'I would like to be a poet', said I. 'To be able to make up stories like the ones you've just told me'.

'Poetry', said he, as if talking to himself. Then to me: 'You are better without that gift, my boy. No-one ever had it without having to pay dear for it. The poet sees a world that the rest of mankind don't. But his soul is sensitive and easily hurt. Be thankful to heaven, boy, for withholding that gift from you. The world would crush you'.

Was there something coming?

'I would ignore the world', I said.

'You couldn't', he replied, 'unless you were alone on a desert island. You must live in a world of men and women who see only the surface of things, and so do not understand the ways and visions of the poet. Let us suppose you had the gift you have wished for. Then after a few years you fell in love with a girl who had no time for your day-dreaming, as she would call it'.

'At long last', said I to myself. 'I have you on the very spot where I wanted you. From this point I will lead you on to tell me your story. It will be great to have it from your own lips. In addition to everything else, it will impress on my nut-brown maid that some men can remain faithful to the memory of an ideal all their life and I will solemnly declare to her that, in Manus Brocach's place, I would do the same thing'.

'No time for your day-dreaming', repeated the old man. 'That was the cause of the trouble between me and my lassie. She hadn't a scrap of interest in the things that meant all the world to me. Often, at my work, aloft in the air, on the scaffolding of a skyscraper, I would get an idea. Then I would spend hours weaving it. I would be so full of it that I wanted to tell it to somebody. And, of course, who else should a man tell a story to but to his wife. Back at home after supper, I would begin to tell it to her. In the middle of it she would begin to tell me about a wonderful bargain she had seen in a downtown store'.

Having heard from Mary Feggy Tammy about this old man's shattered romance, I felt myself losing sympathy for him when I discovered he had married afterwards. He had fallen in my estimation. He was no longer a hero, no longer a martyr to the whole passion of love. Instead of making his saddest thoughts the theme of his sweetest songs, he married another woman to put balm on the lacerated heart after the girl of his dreams had abandoned him. 'Perhaps', I said, 'no man should marry a woman unless he is deeply in love with her'. It was a crude remark, I admit, but I no longer felt pity for him.

'But I was in love with her', said he. 'I loved her with every throb of my heart. Never loved any woman but her, before or after. But that did not save my poor head'.

'What do you mean?' I asked in surprise.

'See that scar?' said he, pointing to his forehead. 'That's where she let me have it with the rolling-pin one evening we were having an argument. But she is dead now. May the Lord have mercy on her'.

'It was a terrible misfortune', I heard myself saying in a dull voice, 'that you did not fall in love with a girl who would understand your ways and appreciate your wonderful gift. There are plenty of such women in the world. I know some of them myself'.

'It is possible, indeed probable', said old Manus, 'that you are convinced you know at least one such woman. Once upon a time I was convinced that I knew another of them. And how I loved her! And what a beauty she was! The fairest flower that ever bloomed. As the song says:

> She was fair and she was charming,
> Pure as the lily in yonder glade;
> Her eyes did glint like the star of morning,
> She was a beauty, was my nut-brown maid'.

Note

1   I am unable to locate any Gaelic version of this story.

INSPIRATION[1]

Conor Ward of Rosmona was in his final year in a teachers' training college when he first got the idea of making a name for himself in literature. It happened in this way. A magazine entitled *The Sunburst* was established in Dublin. Its aim, as stated in the first number, was to turn the thoughts of young Irishmen and women away from what it called the 'play-acting of politicians' and lead them to get their inspiration from the writings of a bygone generation. The *Sunburst* shot over the horizon in a blaze of promise. Why it grew dim after a few numbers and, before a year had elapsed, disappeared from the sky, is not part of our story. It lasted long enough to awaken in Conor Ward the ambition to become a writer.

The first number gave details of a competition for a short story. A prize of three guineas was offered by an Irish American for the best short story dealing with the sea or with a sea voyage. It must not contain less than three thousand words or more than four thousand. The successful story would be published in the magazine in due course and the award would be made on the recommendation of an editorial board whose decision would be final.

Conor Ward wrote a story, sent it to *The Sunburst* and won the prize. A week before he was due to leave the training college, the postman brought him the glad tidings - a copy of the magazine containing his story, a congratulatory letter from the editor and a cheque for three guineas.

Conor was swelling with pride. He showed his story to some of his fellow students. Each of them in turn read it and handed it back without comment. One student, who had competed unsuccessfully, kept spreading the news that the story was not at all an original composition. It was, he maintained, a Gaelic folktale like what one would hear anywhere round the west coast. All Ward did was to translate it. A good enough translation, he admitted. But it was dishonest to pass it off as an original composition, so it was.

Conor brought his story to the principal of the college. The principal read it with evident interest. 'Very good, young man', he said. 'I congratulate you. Very vivid description. At times, I imagined that I saw it all'.

The priest handed the young man back the magazine and then stood up. Was he going to say no more? Offer no further opinion? Give a word of encouragement?

'I intend keeping it up', ventured the student. 'I want to become a writer'.

'It will take time', said the priest. 'I think I am safe in assuming that there are thousands of aspiring writers more favourably placed than you. People who can afford to wait for success. You have to earn your living. Don't take any great risks whatever you do... Good luck and God bless you'.

A week afterwards, Conor left the training college. He came to Derry on the evening train and spent that night in the city. The following day, he went to the Swilly station to take the train home to the Rosses of Donegal.

As he came on to the platform, he heard the call of a newsboy: '*Derry Journal, Derry People, Londonderry Sentinel, Donegal Eagle*'. He bought the *Eagle*, boarded the train and sat beside one of the windows.

After a while, he opened out the newspaper and glanced at the different headings. What he saw did not interest him much. 'Home Rule a virtual certainty. Mr. Devlin addresses huge Hibernian demonstration in Belfast'.

He turned to the local news. Killybegs: big catches of salmon landed the previous week. Rathmullan: work on new pier about to start. The Rosses: here it was at last. The fine success achieved by young Conor Ward of Rosmona. 'We have read his prize-winning story in *The Sunburst* and we have no hesitation in saying that it is a clear signpost on the road to a brilliant literary career'.

The train came as far as Letterkenny. There would be a delay of two hours. The young man walked up the street. He decided to get some tea for himself. But he would not go into the miserable shack with glazed tablecloth and dirty windows where he had often got a mug of tea and a bun for sixpence. He had money in his pocket this time. He would go to the hotel. He might meet with someone who had read *The Sunburst* or, at least, *The Donegal Eagle*.

He went to the hotel and into the dining-room. At one table there was a woman with three noisy children. At another table sat three middle-aged men. One of them Conor knew to be a school inspector. The other two looked and sounded like commercial travellers. They talked about a game of golf they had played at the Rosapenna the previous Sunday, then about a concert that was coming off the following week. They were of one mind on the vocal powers of the police inspector's young daughter. But not one word about the story in *The Sunburst*, or the news item in the *Eagle* announcing the young man who had signposted the road to a brilliant literary career. However, it did not matter. Letterkenny was only a mean, sordid, miserable town!

Later on, Conor was in the train again on his way to the 'Highlands'. He had left the dreary flatlands of the Lagan behind him. The scenery was becoming beautiful, interesting, historic. The train came on to Gartan where Colmcille once played as a child. On past the Rock of Doon where kings had been crowned, and on to the white sandhills of Doe. At last, the wide Atlantic appeared. Tory away on the horizon like a pale, blue cloud ... The train coughed and snorted up the long incline to Falcarragh. Down past the lordly peak of Errigal and on to Gweedore. Rubbleshinny, the next stop, was our traveller's destination ... The train slowed down. At last, it stopped.

There was the big rock as he had left it and the heather glen on the other side.

Our young man alighted. The station-master collected his ticket, asked him was he home for good, but said no more. 'No man', thought Conor, 'is a prophet in his own land. They haven't a word to say about my literary success'.

II

But he was mistaken. The *Donegal Eagle* had come to Rosmona before him and the whole townland had the news. Not alone that but a young man from the place had come from Glasgow on a holiday the day before and he had a copy of the *Sunburst*. Conor Ward's story had been read, listened to, analysed, with some favourable comments, and some not quite so favourable.

As he came to the Cross, he met a middle-aged woman, a relation of his mother. She had a great welcome for him. 'You are a credit to the father and mother that reared you, and to the whole of the parish of the Rosses, from the Ford of Gweedore to the Ford of Gweebarra. We have the *Eagle* at home and all the news about you. Manus was over in Paddy Johnny's yesterday evening. The house was full. The young fellow is just home from Scotland. He read your story for them. Manus says it is great. Sometimes he finds it hard to believe that a neighbour's boy wrote it. You know, a boy like one of our own boys. He says it is like a thing that would be written by a gentleman's son away in some big city. But I remember hearing my grandfather, God rest him, say that it was the Mac Awards made all the songs for the kings long ago, and I told him that'.

Here was appreciation at last. But it was only the beginning. When he arrived home, his mother flung her arms round his neck and wept tears of joy. There was a pile of newspapers on the kitchen table - more than a dozen copies of the *Eagle*.

'What do you want them all for?' asked Conor.

What did they want them for? What else but to send them out to the four corners of the earth - to their people in Scotland, in England, America, Canada etc. Why should they keep the glad news to themselves? Who would keep a lighted candle under a bushel?

'We heard your story read in Paddy Johnny's yesterday evening', said his mother. 'The young fellow brought the book with him from Scotland. I must get one of them to keep'.

As I have said, the story had been read and commented on before the young man arrived home. Some said it was marvellous - that there was a wonderful head on the young man who had written it. But Paddy Johnny's comments on it to another old man later on were not quite so complimentary. 'You know, it isn't everyone I would say it to. And don't you mention it. The poor mother is proud of her child as every mother in her place would be. It would be a cruel blow to tell her the truth. And the truth is that Conor Ward did not make up that story at all. I heard it fifty years ago'.

'What do you mean?'

'Exactly what I say. You remember Felimy Fiddler that used to come round this way long ago. I heard him tell the story more than once. It was about an ancestor of his from Inishmacdurn, Black Fergal O'Boyle, a famous smuggler. One day he went out to meet a Spanish galleon, miles beyond Aran. He loaded his boat with tobacco and rum and made for home. The coastguards in Rosbeg saw him through their spyglasses and went out to get him on the way back. But Fergal O'Boyle led them in among the reefs between Inishmore and the mainland. And he made his way out, leaving the other boat stuck on a rock, for he knew every inch of the ground. The first time I heard that story, I could see Black Fergal O'Boyle ploughing his way through a cloud of spray until he cleared Benmore Headland. I could hear the wind hissing in the shrouds and the shriek of the seagull on the Stags. Hughie Ward's son heard that story. He put English on it and got it put in a book. He got a prize for it. And he gets praised in the papers. But don't mention a word of that. It would be a terrible blow to the poor mother'.

III

'Inniscara school is vacant', said Hughdie Ward to his son. 'It is as good as promised to you. I went over to the parish priest a week ago. He said he would give it to you if no other teacher in the parish applied for it. That means that you have it. For no teacher from the mainland will want a change to one of the islands... It is not what I would like. But it will only be for a few years. I want you to promise me that you will be very careful. Never try to cross the Sound by yourself. The currents on that side of the Rosses are very dangerous'.

'It is no place for him', said the mother. 'If he waits for a while he might get a school in Derry. Is there no other place for him but a miserable island school?'

The young man saw his mother's viewpoint and sympathised with her. But he was reconciled to the island for two reasons. In the first place, he intended to take up writing immediately and what better place for his designs than a quiet island free from distraction. In the second place, there was a charming maiden - little Nellie Boyle from Culbawn. Little Nellie Bawn with her rosy cheeks, her coal-black hair, her eyes like diamonds and her burst of laughter like the lilt of the lark in the clear air. He would meet Nellie on weekends, at least in reasonable weather. And oh, if only she became interested in his literary career! Her influence and her inspiration would enable him to overcome all obstacles.

Conor went to Father O'Donnell, parish priest of the Rosses, a man of about seventy years. 'Yes', said he to the young man, 'your father was here a week ago. I am appointing you to Inniscara school. We can sign the necessary papers later on. You can take up duty on Monday. You will get digs with Mrs. Duffy where your predecessor stayed. A fine woman. She will be like a mother to you'.

He became silent. Had he nothing else to say? Had he not heard of the prize-story in the *Sunburst*? Did he not read the local newspaper? However, he spoke again. 'People born and brought up on the mainland feel lonely on an island. To my mind, there is only one remedy for that - take up some line of study. Let me see, what about working for a degree from the London University? Attendance at lectures not necessary. You can do your work through a correspondence course. Then go to London and sit for the exam. I know one chap who did it. And with his degree he had no difficulty in getting the principalship of a big school in Derry'.

'I intend taking up writing, Father', said the young man.

'Writing? You want to become a journalist?'

'No, Father. I want to write stories, books'.

'What put that idea in your head?'

Good Lord! Had this man never heard of the *Sunburst*? 'It is what I want to do, Father'.

'In that case', said the priest, 'no school or college or correspondence course can do much for you. Nothing but practice, years and years of practice. You must keep at it. Today and tomorrow. This year and next year and next year again. I think it was Pope said it:

> True ease in writing comes from art, not chance,
> As those move easiest who have learned to dance.

'The priest was not very encouraging', said Conor to himself on his way home. He thinks I'll never have the patience to stick it. And, of course, nothing of the help that little Nellie Boyle will be to me.

He decided to go to see his loved one on Sunday afternoon. He was certain she had read the *Eagle*. He would bring her the *Sunburst*. He would unfold his plans to her.

Nellie read the story as the two of them sat in a sheltered nook over the water's edge. She said she liked it and congratulated him on his success.

'I intend to keep on writing', he said.

'Aye, occasionally. It will help to pass the time for you on that lonely island. Please God you will soon get a place on the mainland'.

'Occasionally, did you say? I intend to keep at it day after day and year after year and, in the end, give up teaching and live by my books'.

'But take care you don't ruin your health. After all, you have your work to do as a teacher, and one needs a fair amount of rest and recreation'.

'Wouldn't you like to see six or seven books on a shelf with my name on them?'

'I suppose I would. I am sure I would. But I feel I must warn you against overdoing it'.

This was not very encouraging. It did not give much promise that later on his loved one would encourage him to keep practising day after day and year after year. And then the story in the *Sunburst*. All she said about it was that she liked it. The descriptive passages in it seemed to have made no impression on her. After a few seconds she was talking about something else. Would she change when they were married? He fervently hoped she would.

IV

He went to Inniscara and took up duty. On the afternoon of the first day, as soon as he had taken his dinner, he took pen and paper and began searching his mind for material for a story. An idea would dawn on him. He would think it over. Then he would discard it. Sometimes the core of a story seemed within easy reach of him. Then it would 'break through language and escape'.

But he would keep at it. It was the price he had to pay for fame. The parish priest had told him there was no other way. It was hard. But one day the laurels would be his. If only his darling, bright-eyed Nellie would co-operate. If she had given definite promise of becoming his source of encouragement, his inspiration. But she did not seem to have the least bit of interest in his projects and ambition. But he would keep on without her encouragement, without her inspiration. When he had achieved success, it might waken her ambition!

He kept on writing for about a month and had destroyed the bulk of what he had written. One Friday afternoon he was sitting, writing as usual, when the woman of the house decided to have a word with him.

'Excuse me, master', she began, looking out the window. 'You see that long, thatched house on the brae face - Peter Gallagher's house? I am asking you as a special request to call on that old pair today'.

'I am sorry, Mrs. Duffy', said the teacher, 'I can't go today. Some other time'.

'No other time will do, master. It must be today or not at all'.

'And why today, may I ask?'

'This day fifty years the old pair in that house were married. This is their golden jubilee. Everyone on the island has visited them except yourself. They will be right glad to see you'.

'But I don't know them, Mrs. Duffy', he pleaded.

The woman remained silent for a minute. Then she spoke: 'Pardon me, master, if I say a few words to you that I believe your mother would thank me for saying. You are living here on this island. For the time being it is your home. You are teaching our children. But we want you to be more than a teacher. We want you to be a neighbour as well. If you don't mind my saying it, master, it is wrong to live apart from everybody'.

'All right, Mrs. Duffy. I will call on the old pair', said the teacher, putting away his writing.

V

The teacher went to Peter Gallagher's as requested. There was nobody in the house but the old pair. They were dressed in their Sunday best for the occasion and were sitting one at each side of the fire with a small table between them.

The teacher, feeling somewhat embarrassed, walked up to them, shook their hands and congratulated them.

'Just now we've been talking about you', said the old man, rising to get a chair for the visitor. 'I was wondering would you come'.

'I knew he would come', said the old woman. 'I knew he was a good Christian and, therefore, a good neighbour. You will have a drink with us, master'.

Before he sat down on the proffered chair, the teacher happened to look at the walls. He gasped in wonder at what he saw. The four walls of the kitchen were covered with model boats of all makes and descriptions.

'In the name of heaven, who made all this?' he asked in amazement.

'The two of us, to be exact', replied the old man. 'My hand, sustained and guided by her inspiration. Begin to examine them down there over the door. You will see how crude the first ones are and how they begin to improve after, say, the first seven. Shows you what practice can do. Nothing like it, master'.

'You must have spent a lot of time at it'.

'Every spare hour I had. Stormy days when I could not be out fishing. Rainy days when I could not work on the land. Long winter nights. There are exactly one hundred of them. Two for every year since we got married. I got most of my models from pictures. See that one over the fireplace? That is Lipton's First Shamrock. It took some doing'.

'But where did you get the cordage and the brass rings and the rest of the fittings?'

'Sent to Derry for them. There is a shop in Foyle Street that sells such things... Yes, that one. I had to imagine it. I had nothing to go on except a story my grandfather used to tell long ago. It is supposed to be the boat that Black Fergal Boyle had the day he left the coastguards on the rocks in Inishmore Bay and swept past them under full sail'.

'You are a great man', said the teacher, sitting on the chair. 'The finished article alone proves your skill and your craftsmanship. But that is only what is visible on the surface. Who can gauge the amount of patience and perseverance and endurance put into the work every day for fifty years?'

'But I could not have done it without herself', said the old man. 'She was the inspiration behind it. If it hadn't been for her influence, I wouldn't, couldn't have done it'.

The old woman smiled the gentlest of smiles. 'He is being too generous, master', she said in a faraway voice. 'He is giving me all the credit. But I think he deserves the most of it himself'.

The old man began reminiscing about his life and adventures. 'Many a hard battle I had with the sea, master. The first one was on the day we were married, this day fifty years. In the morning, it was a beautiful day, the most beautiful I remember either before or after. During the day I took a good drop of drink. More, perhaps, than I should have taken. But the day a man gets married to the girl he loves, he is up in the moon. As I have said, the weather was fine in the morning and for part of the afternoon. When we were returning to the island in the evening, the storm burst like a thundercloud. It makes me shudder yet every time I think of it. It was so unexpected'.

'My grandmother, God rest her, warned me not to go to sea that day', said the old woman. 'She said it was only a pet day, that she had known days like it. But I paid no heed to her. Young people are young people, always will be, I suppose. However, we are very glad that you have paid us this visit, master. It is something to remember'.

'My good woman, it will be something for me too to remember. To have seen with my own eyes such unmistakable proof of a long life of love and happiness and harmony'.

'Well, what did you think of them?' asked his landlady when the teacher came back.

'They are a wonderful old pair, Mrs. Duffy', he replied. 'I am very glad that I have paid them a visit and I am thankful to you for suggesting it. He is a wonderful old man. I could hardly believe my eyes when I looked at the collection of model boats. And to think that she was the inspiration behind it all. She must have been a beauty in her young days. There are traces of it still left. And such a gentle, loving creature. And the sound of her voice. So soft and soothing. It is no wonder she exerted such influence over him'.

'She did, indeed, have great influence over him', said the landlady.

'It has done me good to meet them', said the teacher. 'There they are now, in their old age, each of them giving the other the credit for their happiness'.

It was late that night when the teacher slept. He had only one thought in his mind - the influence of a woman on a man's life and actions. He recalled things he had heard or read. What John Mitchel wrote about Mangan's loved-one: 'As a beautiful dream she entered into his existence once for all. As a tone of celestial music she pitched the keynote of his song; and sweeping over all the chords of his melodious desolation you may see that white hand'... Something similar could be said about old Peter Gallagher. All through his splendid display of naval architecture one could see that white hand!

If only little Nellie Boyle would have the same influence over our young teacher he would, he thought, overcome all obstacles and become a successful writer. He must have a few talks with old Peter Gallagher. He must find out how, in his case, the inspiration first made itself felt and how it continued. Could such inspiration be awakened? In other words, could little Nellie Boyle be induced to take an interest in his literary ambitions?

VI

The following day was Saturday and, of course, there was no school. The teacher, looking out through the window, saw old Peter Gallagher hobbling down towards the sea. 'I will follow him down after about ten minutes', said the teacher to himself. He had his career mapped out in his mind. He wanted to become a writer. He believed that the influence of a good woman would be of immense help to him. And old Peter might be able to tell him if such influence could be induced.

When Conor was half-way down, he came to a garden of potatoes, ready to burst into blossom. A cow was in the middle of the plot, doing all the damage that can be imagined. The teacher turned the cow out of the garden and drove her down towards the shore. When he came within sight of the pier, he saw old Peter Gallagher sitting smoking his pipe in the shelter of the breakwater. An excellent spot on such a day. Sheltered from the breeze and facing the sun.

Conor Ward went down to the old man and sat beside him. 'Sorry to disturb you', said he. 'You looked as if you enjoyed being alone. But I want to have a talk with you'.

'Right, master', said the old man. 'But I wasn't alone. I never am on a day like this when I am down here smoking my pipe. I do have my own company but nobody but myself sees them. I see things and I hear things. An odd kind of creature, perhaps, I am. But there you are. Sometimes, as I sit here I see the Land of Youth away on the rim of the ocean. I see it all. The royal palace on the height. The fleet of ships at anchor in the bay. The armies massed on the strands. Sometimes I see Balor going to Tory. Sweeping past Aran Head in a huge ship with her decks bristling with flaming swords. Later on I see Colmcille in a flimsy curragh on his way to conquer the island with no arms but a rough wooden cross. Again I see the treasure ship of the Armada being hurled against the rocks off Mullaghderg. A few days ago I saw Granuaille, the beautiful Queen of the West, as her fleet appeared off Glen Head. She was standing on deck with her golden hair flying in the wind. On her way to invade the Rosses of Donegal, she was. I hated her for that but I could not but admire her beauty and her courage. But you said you wanted to have a talk with me, master'.

'I want to become a writer', said the young man timidly.

'And what advice can I give you? Sure I can't write my name. There was no school on the island when I was a boy'.

'That does not matter. You have done wonderful work. I mean, the model boats. Work that required patience and perseverance'.

'Well, do with the writing what I did with the boats: keep at it'.

'I am trying to, but I am losing heart. After working for a few evenings, I read what I have written. I think it is horrid and I burn it'.

'Never do that, master. Never look back. If I had spent an hour looking at my first model boat, I would see it in all its ugliness. But I did not. I went on and on. Of course, as I have told you, a woman was the driving force behind my perseverance'.

'That is what I want to come to. I intend marrying a girl from Culbawn. A beautiful girl with coal-black hair and eyes like diamonds. Little Nellie Boyle they call her'.

'Well it could happen that little Nellie Boyle will have the same influence on you that my good woman had on me'.

'I don't know. Before I left Dublin, I wrote a story. It was printed. I gave it to her to read. She said she liked it. But that was all she said. She did not give me the least encouragement to keep it up. That disappointed me'.

'Listen, young man', said old Peter, taking the pipe from his mouth. 'The girl you are in love with is one thing, the woman you are married to is another thing. It is only when you are married to her that you realise the force of her influence ...'

Here he was interrupted by the lowing of a cow. He turned around and looked up towards the headland.

'That's my cow', said he. 'I wonder what made her stray down this far'.

'I found that cow in a potato plot on my way down here', said the teacher. 'I turned her out and drove her down to where you see her'.

'Good Lord in heaven!' exclaimed the old man, getting to his feet as fast as his stiff limbs permitted him.

They came to the potato garden. A whole ridge was trampled and half-eaten. It was a sorry sight to see.

'Saviour of Humanity', said the old man. 'What came over me at all, at all? She warned me when I let out the cow to put the stick across the gap in the garden wall. She said it three times. It was the last thing she said as I came out the door ... My God, what a slaughter! It makes me sick to look at it. If it were a fortnight earlier, the damage could be repaired. A good dressing of liquid manure and they would pick up again. But now they are too far advanced. What happened me at all?'

They walked along in silence until they were within a short distance of the house. Then the old man stopped sudden. 'I'll catch it for this, master', he said. 'She'll rip the skin off my bones with her tongue'.

'Who will?' asked the teacher in amazement.

'Who do you think? Who but herself? The woman that God gave me. However, I'll get over it. I have my own shield of defence'.

'Listen', said the teacher. 'I will go in along with you, if you will allow me. I will tell her I met you on the way to the shore. That it was I distracted you and made you forget to put the stick in the gap. Then we will talk about your model boats and of how her inspiration made you persevere'.

'She made me persevere all right', said the old man. The teacher was bewildered. He did not know what to think. It was hard to believe that such a sweet, gentle, old lady who had been her man's lodestar for fifty years should turn round now and scold him for the sake of a handful of potato stalks.

'I am very sorry that this should happen', said the teacher. 'Very sorry to see this little wisp of a cloud in a sky that has been so serene for so long. But, please God, it will soon clear away'.

'Don't you worry, master', said the old man. 'I am well prepared for the fray. I am well used to it. I have the old defence. The defence that has stood me in good stead for the past fifty years. I have a block of wood and my toolbox in the chimney corner ready to start my one hundred and first boat the moment the storm bursts'.

Note

1   I am unable to locate any Gaelic version of this story.

THE LIGHTS OF HEAVEN[1]

He was a young man, a very young man, and he was on his way to meet the girl he loved with every beat of his heart. The season was midsummer, the weather fine, and the scenery superb.

But the young man was not altogether happy. He had decided to make a proposal, to ask a question. What would be the result? Several times before he had made up his mind to declare his love, but he always flinched when the moment came to make the declaration. He often had the words on the tip of his tongue, but he had never managed to utter them.

His darling had a way of reducing him to silence. She always seemed to sense what was on his mind, what he was struggling to put into words. She would begin talking about something miles and miles away from what was in the poor man's mind. And she would keep on talking until he became confused, until he was reduced to stammering incoherent phrases, and finally to silence. But he must say it today. The girl was about to go to Derry to spend some time there with her married sister. What would the result of that visit be? She might take a fancy to the life of the city. And - heart-rending thought - she might take a notion of some young man there and get married.

Some of the girls in her neighbourhood thought Nancy O'Donnell was proud and considered herself a step above them. Her father had a mountain farm which, although not very suitable for tillage, was good for stock-raising. There were only two of them in the family -

herself and her married sister. Nancy could have her choice of the young men of the parish. All she had to do was to get married. Her man would come and live with them, and eventually take over her father's holding.

But that would not satisfy the mother. She wanted to give her remaining daughter a convent-school education. The father did not see much sense in the idea. Time and money wasted, he thought. But in the end the mother had her way. And, at the age of thirteen, Nancy was sent to Erneside convent school. Five years afterwards she came home to Glenmore with all the jewels in her crown - including a gold medal for French.

The mother was very proud of her daughter's French. 'She can speak it the same as I speak Irish', she would say. 'Of course I can't understand a word of it, but I know by the way she rattles it off that it's like second nature to her'.

It is possible that Nancy herself shared her mother's views. But one day after a few months at home she was thoroughly disillusioned. And nothing more was heard about the gold medal.

However, our young man was going to meet her. She had consented to go out cycling with him. She would, of course, go on talking but he would wait patiently until she had finished. Then he would pack what he had to say into a few words. 'Nancy, I love you as never a man loved woman before, and I want you to be my wife'.

He took his bicycle and set out on his journey. When he got as far as the bend in the road at the head of Murlough Bay, he met an old man who was well-known in the Rosses and whom the people called Fergal Feasach. He walked with a stoop, wore a strange kind of cloak and carried a bulky pack strapped to his back. He was on his way down to the lower townlands.

Fergal, although supposed to be 'touched', was reputed to be a man of great learning and deep wisdom. Wouldn't it be a wise thing for a young man in the throes of love and who did not know exactly how to make a declaration that must be made today, wouldn't it be a wise thing to get the advice and opinion of this old philosopher?

The young man came off his bicycle. 'Going down to the seaside, Fergal', he began. 'Down to the seaside. To be exact I am going down to your townland. There will be great pictures in the sky at sunset this evening. And then the changing colours of Errigal. You get a magnificent view of it from Rinnamona'.

He was inclined to walk off without further delay. 'I want to ask you', stammered the young man. 'I want to ask your opinion - your help'.

'Sorry', said Fergal, 'I am in a hurry. I must make sure that I get dry fern to put in my cave. To make a bed for myself, you know. It is a long time since I've been down that way. In any case, if my guess is right, I don't think anyone can help you. You are in the hands of Destiny. Good luck to you'. And he walked away.

II

The young man mounted his bicycle and went on in the direction of Glenmore. The road was not too good. But he should do it in an hour and a half. He would not have to go all the way. Nancy had promised to meet him at the little bridge, about two miles from her home.

He pedalled on, sometimes repeating to himself the declaration of love and the words of the proposal he intended to make. At times he would think about Fergal Feasach. 'The heartless, old wretch. But I know what

happened him. A girl jilted him in his young days. That is
what has made him sour. He is a woman-hater ever since.
But if Nancy says 'yes' this evening - as please God she
will - I will go to him tomorrow and I will tell him about
my happiness. I will burn the heart within him. I will
make him green with envy and jealousy, so I will. And he
deserves it. The cruel, old cynic'.

He rode on for over an hour. At last he came to the
little bridge. He dismounted and sat on the parapet.
Before long he saw a girl on a bicycle coming towards
him. It was Nancy, in all her finery and in all her
blooming beauty.

'Where will we go?' she asked.

'We will go to Claondoire. The view from the side of
the hill will be enchanting this evening'.

Nancy agreed. They mounted their bicycles and set
out. Across through the Windy Gap, up Maghery and on
to Croghy Head. At last they reached the foot of
Claondoire brae. They left their bicycles against the wall
of a cottage by the roadside and proceeded to walk up the
slope, sometimes knee-deep in heather.

When they were halfway up, the young man stopped
suddenly. He had decided on his plan of campaign. 'Just
look at that scene in front of you', he began. 'The blue
ocean away to the Stags of Ros Eoghain, the white sand-
dunes of Leitir, like hills of snow, and the entrance to
Gweebarra Bay. Now look back. Look at Errigal at one
end of the range and the Blue Stack at the other end'.

He was about to turn towards Arranmore and the
chain of islands to the east. But Nancy interrupted him
with her own story. At that moment she knew she was in
love with the young man. She would not, of course, make
the declaration. She would use the traditional method.
She would tease him for a while. She would talk about

everything and anything for a spell. That would annoy him. It would confuse him. For a time she would ignore all his hints. At last she would provoke him into saying what she wanted him to say.

'Do you know who spent last week with us?' she began. 'Feargal Feasach. I think he is gone down your way today. He is very interesting. A marvellous story-teller. I could listen to him for days on end. Some people think he is mad. That is because they can't understand him. Others say he is one of the Simeys - the tinker tribe from Glenswilly. As a matter of fact he comes from Tyrone. A place called Monterlunny, where they still speak Irish'.

'Nancy, we won't meet again for five weeks', interrupted the young man - giving a clear hint that they had more important things to settle than the life story of a wandering beggar.

'Tinker indeed', said Nancy. 'Where do you think a tinker learned Latin and French and all the other subjects? But I know the whole story and I'll tell you how I got to know it.

'It doesn't matter. I believe you without any proofs'.

'Last year as you know I got a gold medal for French in the Intermediate'.

'And the people of the parish were all very proud of you'.

'My head was a bit swelled over my success, and my mother was worse'.

'You were entitled to your bit of a swelled head. But will you listen to me, Nancy?'

'As I was saying when you interrupted me, I was very proud of my gold medal. As for my mother, nothing would do her but that I would go over to the parish priest and show it to him. I got on my bicycle and cycled to Glenlocha. When I came to the parochial house the priest was at the gate talking to a man who was standing on the road. Who was it but Fergal'.

Each of them saluted me. Then they resumed their conversation. They were talking in a strange language. I could not understand a word of it. I took it to be Latin'.

'It possibly was. But would you mind, Nancy ...'.

'Please don't interrupt me. After about five minutes Fergal touched his hat and walked away'.

'Did you want to see me, Miss O'Donnell?' asked the priest.

''Well yes, Father, I did', says I. 'It is about my future career. My mother would like your opinion on whether I should go on for teaching or for nursing''.

''A lot should depend on your own choice', says he. 'Also on your standard of education. By the way, how did you get on in your examination?'

''Good Lord', says I to myself, 'has this man never heard of my gold medal for French? But he will hear''.

The young man opened his mouth in an attempt to make one more effort to stop her rigmarole but he was utterly confused and could not say a word.

'The priest looked after Fergal who was going down the road', continued Nancy. 'Poor Fergal', says he. 'He was a genius, if ever there was one. He was my classmate for four years in the Irish College in Paris. One day he went out and did not return. He discovered he had no vocation. Keep that to yourself', says he. 'You know how ignorant people sometimes look on what they call a spoiled priest. But', says he, 'he had the brains. A marvellous linguist he was. He has retained his French much better than I have. You may have noticed how fluent he was while I was getting bogged at every second sentence'.

'I did not produce my gold medal. I did not mention it. Never will. Neither will my mother. That chapter is closed'.

III

She had teased him enough, she thought. Perhaps too much so. He seemed dazed. Still she was fairly confident that in the end she would make him say what she wanted him to say.

'Well, right enough', she said, 'the view from here is superb … Enough to make anyone feel happy. Life has its great moments'.

He made no reply. Was it because he was dull-witted, or had she teased him too much? But she would continue the attack.

'By the way', she said, 'I meant to give you back your book today'

'Which book?'

'*Moore's Melodies*'.

'You can keep it. Keep it forever'.

'You are very good. I love *Moore's Melodies*. There is one in particular that springs to my mind just now as I look across the sea to Glen Head. "I saw from the beach"'.

> I saw from the beach when the morning was shining
> A bark o'er the waters move gloriously on,

he began to quote, but the girl interrupted him. 'That is not the verse that appeals to me', she said, determined on bringing her heavy artillery into action. 'No, but these lines:

147

Oh, who would not welcome that moment's returning
When passion first waked a new life through his frame
A moment like this when earth becomes a fairyland.

He no longer hesitated. He clasped her to his bosom. Their lips met. Their souls fused into one. Earth looked like heaven.

'I am too happy', said Nancy later on. 'Is this only a dream? ... Will you always love me, Shamey?'

'What an absurd question to ask. Don't you know I'll always love you'.

'Even when I am old and grey and full of sleep and nodding by the fireside'.

'For heaven's sake, Nancy, don't talk nonsense'.

Then they said all the little nothings that only true lovers say to one another.

'I loved you, Shamey, from the first time we met and that is over a year ago'.

'And, you little fairy, you kept me on burning coals for what seemed an eternity. Talking about Fergal Feasach'.

'That was only to test you. To make sure that you really loved me. I'd have kept it up longer only I saw the look of pain and anguish on your face. Then I knew you loved me with all your heart'.

They came down to the road, took their bicycles and set out for Nancy's home. The sun had gone down on the western horizon but its rays were coming through the Windy Gap, filling the valley below with a flood of golden light.

They cycled on until they reached the bottom of the slope, a few hundred yards from Nancy's home. 'I think I'll walk the rest of it', she said. 'It is a bit steep and I am getting tired'.

They dismounted. Shamey looked at his love. 'This day five weeks we'll meet again, please God', he said. 'I'll be counting the hours, not to say the days'.

'Won't you come up to the house?' said Nancy. 'You will want a bite to eat before starting off again. And I am sure that neither my father nor my mother will have the slightest objection'.

He would, of course, go in. He was only too glad to be asked.

'You may find my father and mother a bit strange in ways', said Nancy as they walked along beside their bicycles. 'They love one another very much. Yet in ways they are very different in outlook. Each has his own way of looking at the affairs of the nation. My father was only seven years old when his family was evicted in Glenveagh - thrown on the roadside in the snows of winter, to watch their little home being smashed to bits by the battering-ram. They all had to emigrate. When my father grew up and had earned some money, he came back and bought this place. My father is what you might call a child of the Land War'.

'And your mother?' queried Shamey.

'My mother is a child of the Fenian movement. Her father's house was in Derry. He was in the I.R.B. When all was lost in '67 he went to the States. It was there he met my grandmother. She came from Crobawn, away in the direction of Lough Finn. In due course they came back to Ireland and settled in Crobawn. Now you will understand why they sometimes differ on national issues. I never interfere in their discussions, although my sympathies are on my mother's side. However, they love one another, and that is the main thing'.

'Of course it is', agreed Shamey. And then added: 'I could not imagine you and me holding different views on anything'.

They came to the house and went in.

Nancy's father, a strongly-built man past middle-age, sat in the chimney corner placidly smoking his pipe. The mother was on the other side, reading a book. She too was past middle-age. She was neatly dressed, and she was still good-looking. A table with a white cloth on it stood in the corner of the kitchen and the kettle was singing on the hearth.

'You must be dead hungry', said the mother when the introductions were over. Then she got up and set the table for four.

The supper was soon ready. And what a supper for a hungry pair. Stacks of scones, and oaten bannock, butter, cream, honey. All home produce.

Shamey wanted to say something. 'You have a fine place here, good luck to you', he said.

'The land around here looks poor', said the father. 'But it is good for stock-raising. Excellent for mutton. Limestone bottom, you know. Down in the lower hills it is the same land in appearances. But it is no good. Granite bottom, you know. Makes all the difference in the world'.

At the first pause the mother changed the conversation. She mentioned her married daughter who lived in Derry. Had spent a few weeks there the pervious summer. Liked it very much. Supposed it was partly due to the fact that Derry was her father's native city.

'We went to Dublin for a few days, Bridie and myself', she continued. 'We went to the Abbey to see *Kathleen Ni Houlihan*. It is a great play. So sad. Yet at the same time so full of hope'.

This was the way to entertain young folk. Something in keeping with the spirit of the enlightened age - and not talk about the value of limestone bottom for sheep-rearing. And if she could only bring the conversation round to her daughter's gold medal for French, it would crown the festival. But Fergal Feasach had destroyed that illusion. Nancy thought of it too. It was a pity. But she consoled herself. She had been asked to pilot a group of Rosses women to Lourdes the following summer. The bubble would surely burst then. It was better to have it burst where there was nobody to witness her embarrassment and humiliation!

Later on the man of the house took a lantern and went out to have a look at the cowhouse and the stable. This was a grand opportunity for the mother to make an impression on Shamey. She had the stage to herself. 'I cried when I saw O'Connell Street in ruins', she began. 'But then I dried my eyes. I knew, and I do know, that there will be another day. Ireland has a leader this time. A brand from the fires of Easter Week … Yes, I could feel it in Dublin. In the words of Pearse, Ireland has been rebaptised in the Fenian faith. The Fenian faith was nearly dead'.

She was so excited that she did not hear her husband's footsteps coming back from the outhouses.

'Yes, it was nearly dead', she went on. 'The Land League folk all but killed. They made Irishmen adopt a new slogan and forget the old one. They put 'The Land for the People' in the place of 'Ireland for the Irish''.

'Black Polly won't calve the night', said her husband, blowing out the lantern. 'She is lying there as quiet as you like'.

It was after midnight when Shamey left for home. He cycled down the glen, and on to where the road skirts the lake. All of a sudden he saw a light shooting across, over the surface of the water. He came off his bicycle and stood watching the light until it disappeared on the far shore. He recalled having read somewhere that certain birds carry a phosphorescent glow in their wings. But he dismissed it as 'book-nonsense' and soon found himself firmly believing the fairy-stories of his childhood days. That was a fairy on its way to the Palace at Breenach. He could imagine the Palace with its thousand lights.

When he reached home he looked at his watch. It was two o'clock. He decided he would not go in and go to bed. Why would he bury himself in a small poky bedroom with its one-pane window, and that not even facing the moon.

He put his bicycle in an outhouse and went down towards the sea. The moon was full and there was not a wisp of cloud in the sky. He looked towards the South. The Hills of Donegal stood like huge sentinels, dark against the sky. A star seemed poised on the peak of Errigal. Shamey recalled something he had read about Mont Blanc as seen at sunrise from the Vale of Chamouni.

'Hast thou a charm to stay the morning-star?'

He stood and listened to the croon of the bar, and the ripple of the wavelet on the strand. Murmurs that seemed to enhance the silence instead of disturbing it.

Suddenly he looked across the creek and he saw a figure moving among the sand-dunes. Who could it be? Perhaps someone out robbing rabbit snares. It was a mean form of robbery. But it was no business of a man in love, was loved in return, and was there on the lonely shore to dream about his happiness under the magic spell of the moon.

But the figure was coming towards him. Could it be possible? It was. It was Fergal Feasach.

'What are you doing out at this hour of the morning?' called Shamey when they came within earshot.

'I'll tell you that later on', replied Fergal sitting on a boulder. 'Or rather it will tell itself. Don't sit on the grass. Sit on this stone here. There is a heavy dew … You ask what I am doing out at this hour. It is a habit of mine on summer mornings in fine weather. But now might I ask what you are doing out?'

'I'll tell you', replied Shamey, only too glad to have the opportunity of talking about his dear one. 'I am in love, and in return I am loved'.

'I guessed that when we met yesterday. And I guessed who the girl was. I heard your name mentioned more than once'.

'But you wouldn't help me', said Shamey good-humouredly. 'I wanted your advice on the best way to make a declaration. In reply you said something about the golden castles that would be in the sky at sunset, and you walked away'.

'Listen, child', said Fergal, 'for that is all you are. I had no advice to give you. I knew that if the girl loved you it did not matter how you worded your declaration. You could babble like a child learning to talk and she would accept your proposal. On the other hand if she did not love you all the eloquence of a Demosthenes would fail to make an impression on her. However, I know by you that she has said 'yes'. I know you are happy'.

'Happy! I can't find words to describe my happiness'.

'Nobody can describe his own happiness', said Fergal.

'Language was given to us for expressing commonplace thoughts. But we are dumb when faced with the task of expressing the emotions of the heart - whether gladness or sadness, happiness, sorrow, anger, remorse. But listen', he said, holding up his hand. 'Not a murmur out of you'.

All of a sudden the sky thrilled to the warbling of countless birds. There seemed to be millions of them ... The music lasted for about ten minutes. Then it stopped as suddenly as it had begun.

'That is what I came out to hear', said Fergal. 'The birds greeting the dawn. Like the heavenly hymn of a choir of angels. Now that it is all over, try to describe it. You can't. Nobody can. You are in love with a beautiful girl. Even in my neutral eyes she is beautiful. She is a million times more so in your eyes. But try to describe her beauty. You cannot make the faintest attempt at it. Oisín was the greatest of our ancient Gaelic poets. Yet, when asked by St. Patrick to describe the beauty of Niamh, all the poor bard could say was, 'Patrick, if you had seen her you would have fallen in love with her yourself'. It is the same with every other emotion. When Othello looked at the beautiful face of Desdemona dead, when he realised her innocence, and the enormity of his own crime, how did he express the soul-shaking remorse he felt for having murdered her? Centuries afterwards one Bill Shakespeare alleged that the poor fellow implored the devils to whip him from the possession of so heavenly a sight, to blow him about in the winds, to roast him in sulphur, to wash him in steep-down gulfs of liquid fire. The poet's words may give us an idea, if only a faint one, of the murderer's remorse. But we can be sure that Othello never said a word of it. He said nothing. He threw himself on the ground and howled like a wounded dog. Then he killed himself'.

Fergal became silent for a while. At last he said: 'There's the dawn'. He got up and walked down to the edge of the sea.

'Not a particle of it left', said he when he came back. 'All gone. Towers, battlements, mail-clad sentries'.

'What do you mean?' asked Shamey in amazement.

'Five or six little lads who spent hours there in the creek yesterday afternoon building a sand-castle. The tide has swept it all away. The little fellows are asleep in their beds now, perhaps dreaming about this fortress. Later on they will come running down, to find nothing but a slight swelling in the sand. However, they were happy while they were building it … I could have told them that the tide would roll in while they were asleep and sweep away their castle'.

'Why didn't you? It would save them from the cruel disappointment that is in store for them'.

'Why should I tell them?' asked Fergal. 'They were happy. Why should I put out the lights of heaven on the poor things? I think I will go now and have a few hours sleep'.

'Won't you come in later on for a bite to eat?'

'I have plenty of food in my cave thanks to your good mother. Bread, butter, tea, everything. And I have heaps of driftwood to make a fire … I am glad that your love affair has come to a successful issue. You are getting a grand girl. Good morning now, and may God bless you'.

Shamey came up to the house. But he did not go in and go to bed. He sat on a rock. The world was beautiful. There was gladness in the smile of the rising sun as it rose over the peak of Errigal.

V

The next time Shamey went to see Nancy he went by car - a car owned and driven by a young man named Donal Boyle.

'Where does she live?' asked Donal as they set out.

'In a townland called Glenmore on the road to Doochary. I'll direct you as we go along'.

They drove on in silence - across a mountain road to Clochglas, on to Benroe, turned left and through the Windy Gap and on to Glenmore.

'You see the whitewashed house on the side of the brae', said Shamey. 'That is where she lives'.

When they came opposite the house Donal stopped the car. The two men got out and proceeded to walk up a laneway towards the house. When they were within about a score of yards of the door a young girl came out carrying a turf basket. Shamey was overcome with emotion. He ran towards her with outstretched arms. 'Nancy, darling', he exclaimed. She backed away from him for some distance. Then she faced him with a look of fear and wonder in her eyes. 'My name is not Nancy', she said.

Shamey recovered from his confusion. 'I am very sorry', said he, 'very sorry indeed. I thought you were Nancy O'Donnell. You are so like her'. And he made known his identity to the girl.

'Wait there a moment', she said. 'I want to put a few sods of turf on the fire and see if the bread in the oven is baked. Then I will take you to Nancy O'Donnell. I'll be back to you in about five minutes'.

'Isn't she a beauty?' said Donal when the girl had gone into the house. 'Never, never, in all my life have I seen such a beautiful face'.

After about five minutes the girl returned. 'My bread is not quite baked yet', she said. 'Will the two of you come in for a little while?'

'We are alright here, thanks', said Shamey.

'Come on in', said Donal. 'There will be a downpour in a few minutes. See that black cloud over Sliabh Gorm. It will be down on top of you before you know where you are'.

The two men went inside along with the girl. The only other person in the house was an old woman who sat in a low chair in the chimney-corner. A chair was put down for Shamey beside her. Shamey looked at her and as he did he thought she was the ugliest old woman he had ever seen. The skin on her neck and throat hung down like a limp rag. Her fingers were gnarled and twisted from arthritis. Her mouth was open showing her worn, toothless gums.

Shamey was uneasy. He did not want to sit beside the ugly old hag. Would he excuse himself to the girl and say he would look for someone else to take him to Nancy O'Donnell? He was about to do so when the old woman turned her face towards him and began to talk.

'They told me he was coming', she began. 'He will never come. Yesterday I sat at the window all day watching out for cyclists coming up the Windy Gap. Quite a lot of them came. But they all passed the gate, one after another … He will never come. He is not free to come. He is behind prison bars. They came one morning at dawn, they came with guns and bayonets and they took him away … Dreadful things are happening … Last week I followed poor Plunkett O'Boyle[2] down the Glen to a lonely graveyard in Cruit. They murdered him in cold blood. Many's the night he spent in this house. And then

Charlie Daly and his three comrades. They had come to us from Munster to pay back in some measure the debt due to Tírchonaill for having once marched to Kinsale. And they were shot like mad dogs would be shot, over there in Drumboe a few days ago. Shot by a firing squad of Irish speakers from the Gaeltacht. The language of Ireland is being revived ... The will of the people! What kind of people? Some bribed, some frightened. How can such people have a will? ... Thank God we have the Chief. He will never take an oath of allegiance to the King of England. He will never have anything to do with their Free State. He said it in plain words down in Kerry last Patrick's Day'. "While grass grows and water runs I will not enter a twenty-six county parliament"'.

Shamey wanted to get away. He had no desire to sit there looking at the ugly, old woman and listen to her mad ramblings. Still, he was sorry for her. In a way he felt glad that she had kept one of her illusions, and he hoped it would remain with her until her last breath.

She became silent. Shamey looked sideways at her. A frightful change had come over her. There was a wild mad look in her eyes. Her mouth was drawn tight. Her fists were clenched so tightly that the knuckles showed white. She began again, in a husky voice.

'I grieve for them all. For Plunkett O'Boyle, for the Dromboe prisoners, for Rory, Liam, Dick and Joe. Grieve for them with sorrow in my heart. But it is a kind of sweet sorrow as the man said. But the other sorrow It would make me commit murder. The sorrow I feel for Paddy McGrath and Charlie Kerins, and the men who died on hunger-strike ... All is gone. Gone forever. Now we are told that the ideals we cherished for centuries were only an empty formula'.

'Excuse me', said the young girl to Donal. 'I think your

car is not far enough in from the middle of the road'. And as she went out along with Donal she made a sign to Shamey to follow them.

'I am sorry', she explained when they were outside, 'but when she goes off on that tack she could become delirious and remain so for days. I've seen it happen before, more than once. The only thing to do is to leave her to herself for about a quarter of an hour. Then she will become quite normal again'.

'Listen, my good girl', said Shamey. 'We won't disturb you any longer. You can go in and look after her when you think fit. If you would be good enough as to tell me where Nancy O'Donnell lives'.

'I am sorry for not having explained, but the old woman in there is Nancy O'Donnell'.

'That …!' exclaimed Shamey in stark amazement.

'That, whatever you feel you must call her'.

'I am sorry. Very sorry … I think, in God's name, we'll go, and not disturb her anymore'.

'That would hardly be fair, since you have come to see her', said the girl. 'In a few minutes when she gets her memory back she will remember everything. And she will want to talk to you. By the way, what happened to you when you ran to me and called me 'Nancy'?'

'I could not exactly describe it. I got all confused. The past took the place of the present. Fifty years of my life vanished like lightning. I was young again. Now that I realize that it was only a flashback makes me sad. So sad that I would rather not go in again'.

'You cannot go away like that, uncle', protested Donal. 'You must go back in to see her'.

The three of them went back into the house. The old woman had quite recovered in the meantime. Shamey sat on a chair beside her. She looked at him and held out her hand. He took it and raised it to his lips, very much against his inclination. It was the withered, old hand of a withered, old woman.

'So you did come to see me', she said. 'It was very good of you after all the long years. I appreciate it very much. When Nellie told me you were outside I was very glad. Then I got mixed-up as I sometimes do. I am sure I talked a lot of nonsense. But I am all right again. And I am glad to see you'.

'I never forgot you, Nancy', said he. 'I have been making enquiries about you all the time. And I was very sorry a few years ago when I heard that your good man died'.

'He was a good man', she replied. 'A good father and a good husband. You would never be lonely when he was about. He had something to say about everything, some story to tell. And we loved each other very much. It was the right kind of love. The love that marriage should be based on, not the …'

She paused for a little while.

'That evening on Claondoire brae fifty years ago', she resumed, 'was not a foundation for marriage. It was only a dream … Still I can't forget it … I would like to live it over again. I can't explain myself'.

'But even if fate had not separated us, you would not have married me?' he probed.

'To be candid with you I don't believe I would', she replied. Then she looked at him as if she were examining every feature of his face. 'No I would not', she said. 'I would have chosen Paddy. I am certain of that now'.

'Good Lord', he thought, 'there are two of us in it. I too am old and ugly'.

'But', he protested, as if feeling slighted, 'you still dream about the evening on Claondoire brae'.

'I do', she said. 'And I would like to live it over again. You understand me now. You remember the lines I quoted you that day.

> Oh, who would not welcome that moment's returning
> When passion first waked a new life through his frame.

'Very good, Nancy', he said. 'It will return. We'll be young again. We'll be together in heaven. And we'll ask permission to come back to earth for a spell and revisit Claondoire brae'.

This idea seemed to make her glad, although she treated it as a joke. 'My old man might be lonely in my absence', she said.

'We will leave my old woman with him to keep him company while we are away', suggested Shamey.

'He would bore the life out of her. He was a terrible talker. You could not get a word in edgeways with him'.

'Don't you worry', said Shamey. 'He is going to meet his Waterloo this time'.

She smiled faintly. 'It was kind of you to come to see me', she reflected. Then she became silent. At last she leaned back in the chair and closed her eyes ... They soon knew by her breathing that she was asleep. Was she dreaming? We don't know. And if she was, what was it about? We don't know. Perhaps of 'that moment's returning'.

'I think you could go now', said the girl. The three of them went outside. 'Thanks again for your visit. I must be off now. I want to be with her when she wakens'.

VI

The two men got into the car and drove off. Both of them were silent. Each of them was dreaming. The young man of the image that had just come into his life. The old man saddened by the memory of a vanished dream.

Coming along Glenmore Shamey noticed rocks and bushes darting past him like swallows. He looked at the speedometer: the needle was trembling at sixty. 'Excuse me, Donal', he said as calmly as he could. 'I want to get out for a moment'.

Donal slowed down, and finally brought the car to a halt.

'I did not want to get out', said the old man, 'but I was afraid to shout at you. Do you know that you were doing sixty miles? Sixty miles on this road!'

'I am very sorry, uncle, very sorry. But I don't know what I was doing. My head is in the clouds'.

'Well, take it down out of the clouds, if you don't want to get it smashed, and mine along with it'.

'Listen, uncle. Keep your eye on the speedometer and don't let me go over thirty'.

They drove on. Through the Windy Gap. Down into the Lower Rosses, and along the coast road in the direction of Gweedore. When they came to the 'Heather Bar' at the head of Murlough bay the driver stopped the car. 'We'll go in and have a drink', he said.

'I am not in the humour for drinking'.

'Come on in, man, and have sense. A drink will buck you up. And you need bucking up if I know anything'.

They went into the pub.

'Do you know', said Donal sipping his drink, 'that is the most beautiful girl I ever saw. Dazzling, I say she is'.

'Could be the operative word, Donal'.

'Listen, uncle. I want to go up to Glenmore again next Sunday. Will you come with me?'

'Sorry, Donal, I can't. I just can't. Please don't ask me. Can't you go on your own?'

'No, I can't. I had a word with her on the quiet. She has no objection to my visit. But she prefers that I should have some old or elderly person along with me. She wants the neighbours to believe it's someone visiting the old woman. That is why I am asking you to go, uncle'.

'I told you I can't go. I am sorry but I can't and that's that'.

'I wonder would auntie come with me?'

'I don't know. She might. You were always a pet of hers. Besides, she might be curious to see this dream girl of mine. Women have strange fancies at times'.

They arrived at the hotel in Coteen where Shamey and his wife were spending a few weeks' holidays. They went into the small lounge. Shamey's wife was there by herself, reading a book.

'In the name of God, where have the two of you been gallivanting all day? Tea is over an hour and a half ago. However, I suppose I must go to the kitchen and see what they can do'.

'Do, get some tea for us, auntie, please', said the young man. 'In the meantime I'll order a drink. What is everybody having?'

'Listen, auntie', said Donal, 'she just swept me off my feet. I am head over ears in love with her'.

'You are being mysterious, Donal', said the old woman.

'I thought I told you, auntie. I didn't? I am all upset, so

I am. But she is a beauty if there ever was one'.

'But in God's name, who is she?'

'Nancy O'Donnell's granddaughter', said Donal. And he told auntie the whole story of their visit to Glenmore. 'And I am not without hope', he concluded. 'She gave me a few hints that made it pretty clear that she had no objection to meeting me again. I want to go there next Sunday'.

'Well, go and see her. What is to stop you?'

'I can't go by myself', he explained. 'Will you come with me?'

'What would I be doing going along with you? Get your uncle Shamey to go'.

'I asked him. I implored him. But he won't come. Says he can't. Says he has taken his farewell look at Nancy O'Donnell, and does not want to see her again - at least in this world'.

'I see the play is finished for him', said the old woman. 'Someone has said 'they have their exits and their entrances'. You are coming on the stage, Donal. He is gone off. He is down among the audience'.

'My exit from the scene of my youth', said the old man in a sleepy voice. 'I made that years ago. Only today I went to look at the old theatre. There was nobody there but a withered old woman crouched over a guttering stump of a candle. There were neither actors nor audience. The hall was empty. The lights were fled, the garlands dead'.

'I will go with you to Glenmore next Sunday, Donal', said the old woman. 'If it were only to tell poor old Nancy O'Donnell how lucky she was not to be married to that sour old cynic. If you come here after lunch on Sunday. Say three o'clock'.

'That will suit me grand', said the young man getting to his feet. The old woman stood up at the same time. 'Good night, uncle Shamey', said Donal to the old man. Then he looked lovingly and gratefully at the old woman. He put an arm around her and kissed her affectionately.

'You are my Guardian Angel, auntie Connie', he said.

She went to the door with him.

'He has it bad', she said when she came back.

'Are you really going with him to Glenmore on Sunday?' Shamey asked her.

'Of course I am. Why wouldn't I?'

'But listen to me, Connie … '.

'Not a word out of you. Would you put out the lights of heaven on the poor boy?'

'Put out the lights of heaven', said Shamey. 'Where did I hear those words before?'

To himself he said the rest as he lay back in the chair and closed his eyes. 'I wonder if the lot of mankind would not be happier if what some people call the lights of heaven had never been lit?'

Notes

1 I have been unable to discover any Gaelic original for this story. The specific references in this story to executions of Republicans during the Civil War never occur in any of the author's Gaelic short stories even though he sometimes uses the backdrop of the Civil War in some of them.

2 Plunkett O'Boyle, a close friend of Séamus Ó Grianna and his family, fought on the Republican side in the Civil War and was killed at the end of that war. An account of this incident is reported in the *Irish Independent*, 16.5.23, 7 and 17.5.23, 7. Pádraig Ó Baoighill details the history of the armed struggle in Donegal and gives a detailed biography of Plunkett in his book *Óglach na Rosann: Niall Pluincéad Ó Baoighill* (Coiscéim, 1994).

THE ROSSES REVISITED[1]

Black Jimmy Boyle, living in Glasgow with his family for over thirty years, decided to have one last look at the hills of Donegal. He would go to his native Glenmore in the Rosses. He would visit all the places associated with his boyhood, youth and early manhood. Perhaps he would dream his day-dreams over again and for a brief spell – forget that the bright hopes he and others had once cherished went down in disaster and woe. Above all places he would visit the ruins of *Cúirt na hÉigse*, the ancestral home of the McGilligans and, for generations, the pride of the Rosses.

At this stage a description of Glenmore and an account of some of those who inhabited it are necessary to the understanding of our story. The glen is over three miles long with a river running through it. This river rises in Loughnanillan, meanders through the upland for a few miles until it enters the head of the glen. From there it flows along at varying degrees of speed until it enters the sea at the head of the Dobhar inlet. To the North-east of the head of the inlet a high promontory about three hundred yards long juts into the sea.

The McGilligans originally came from the rich lands of the banks of the Erne. When the plantation began they were forced to move westwards. Bit by bit they retreated. Manus Garbh McGilligan was the first of the clan to venture into the wilds of the Rosses. That was early in the eighteenth century.

Manus came to Glenmore and decided to build a house on the tip of the promontory. It would be exposed to the storm, his wife warned him. It would be much better, she said, to build it in a sheltered spot a mile or so up the glen. Manus countered her suggestion by saying that the glen would have little sunshine, and therefore would not be good for children. Children, he contended, needed lots of sunshine, to make them strong and healthy and happy. 'Besides', he added, 'children need beautiful surroundings, beautiful scenery. And what more beautiful spot than the tip of the promontory?'

He built a low house and roofed it with thatch. His idea of a thatch roof was what he was used to – triangular gable-end peaks and scalloped thatch. He would have built and roofed the house according to his notion if he had not been put wise by a man from an outside district who one day wandered down as far as the glen. The visitor advised Manus Garbh to change his plan. A house built and roofed in such a way, he said, would not survive one winter. The gable-ends must be round, so as to give a round roof. The thatch must be kept in place, not by scallops, but by ropes going right over the roof, about six inches apart and fastened to stone pegs along the eaves. And there was the knob known as the *cabar*, so that if one length of rope happened to break the other lengths were as secure as ever.

Manus built a spacious kitchen first. In the course of time he added more to it – bedrooms, barn, stable, etc. When finished, it was close on a hundred feet long. Viewed from a certain spot, in a certain light and against the background of the sea, it was like a long, low ship sailing away towards the sunset.

But how did it come to be known as *Cúirt na hÉigse*, or the Palace of Poetry? That appellation came at a later date when the glen became populated. And there was a good reason for it.

Manus Garbh claimed to be a direct descendant of Diarmuid Mac Giollagáin who, in bygone ages, used to play the harp in the banquet hall of Donegal Castle. 'The same Diarmuid was a poet as well as a musician', Manus would say. 'Poetry runs in families, but it is not continuous. It does not come from father to son. It goes to sleep for generations. Then it wakens out again. I suppose it is in the heart all the time, although the tongue can't utter it. My grandfather, Niall Roe, was the last poet of the tribe. Composed very beautiful songs. Poetry could break out anytime now'.

It did break out but not until the third generation after Manus Garbh. Black Patrick McGilligan had three sons and they composed beautiful poetry in their day. It was then the long, thatched cottage on the promontory came to be called *Cúirt na hÉigse*.

The *Cúirt* was a solid edifice. Its walls were thick and strong. The thatch was tied down and kept in place with ropes made of shavings of bog fir – the only kind of rope that could stand the stress of the storm and would not become rotted by the rain and the salt spray of the sea.

But one night in January 1839 a storm blew that had no parallel in recorded history. All the houses along the west coast of Donegal had their roofs blown off. Except those built in sheltered nooks. In the morning there was nothing left of the *Cúirt* except the bare walls.

But it got a new lease of life. The McGilligans got to work. They dug up new logs of bog fir. They cut them into rafters and laths and placed them in position. On top of this rib-work they put a layer of scraws. Over the scraws they spread the thatch and tied it down with strong ropes.

The generation of McGilligans in the glen at that time were very proud of their regenerated *Cúirt*. They had a banquet to celebrate the occasion. They sang their own native songs. The man of the house thanked the neighbours who had helped to make the feast a success. The *Cúirt* could not be destroyed, he said. Its history and tradition would live forever. So would the songs composed on its hearth by the sons of Black Patrick – Aodh, Séamus and Peadar![2]

II

For fifty-odd years after the night of the Big Wind the *Cúirt* continued to flourish. True, no new generation had as yet come to walk in the footsteps of Black Patrick's sons. But their songs continued to be sung throughout the Rosses, at weddings and christenings and wakes. They sang the song about the Glenmore cow that was sold to a man in Tory and swam back to the mainland, following the example of Balor's famous Glas Ghaibhleann. The song about the night the fairy host came sweeping down the heathery slopes of Meenagee, took a boat from the creek of Rinnamona and sailed across the sea to Spain to tell the ghost of Red Hugh that all had not been lost at Kinsale. And, for the wake, there was the heart-rending lament of a father over the body of his drowned son.

The traditions of the *Cúirt* were honoured and preserved. And except that a schoolhouse had been built and that the menfolk began to go across to Scotland for seasonal work, there was very little change in the pattern of life in Glenmore.

But at last war-clouds began to gather on the horizon, and stories began to circulate – for there was as yet no newspaper coming to the Glen. There was the story of the one-armed man from Mayo who had spent ten years a prisoner in an English dungeon, and who managed to keep his sanity by working out a plan for the destruction of landlordism in Ireland. The people of Glenmore did not use English as their everyday speech. But they had heard the famous phrase 'keep a firm grip on your homesteads', and they took their own meaning out of it. Then the example of how to keep the grip was coming to them from the neighbouring parish of Gweedore where the Parish Priest, Father McFadden, was leading his people in a campaign of resistance to landlordism which has since become part of the history of Ireland.

In due course the weight of coercion in the Rosses was directed to Glenmore. Demands were sent out for arrears which the people thought had been allowed to lapse, and which many of them were unable to pay, consequent on the failure of the crops for two consecutive seasons.

The first place singled out for attack was the *Cúirt*. And what better place to encourage the will to resist? The first and most revered residence in the Glen. The house of loving and proud memories.

Neil McGilligan, the then occupant, was served with a notice to pay his arrears. He was served with a second notice. He ignored both. Then came the third and final notice, stating that if the 'amount due' was not paid before a specified date, the occupant would be evicted.

The men of the Glen were ready. In due course the bailiff, accompanied by two policemen, came to enforce the law. But when they saw the resistance they had to contend with they decided to postpone the operation. After a few days the bailiff came back again, this time accompanied by over a dozen of armed policemen. Their opening attack was an attempt to force open the door. But here they met with a form of defence – or rather counter-attack – they did not expect, boiling gruel poured from a hole made in the roof.

The battle went on for a long time. The police fired several rounds at the door and windows, but the bailiff could not gain admission. The 'Gweedore ammunition', was keeping them at bay.

At last an ultimatum was shouted to them giving them five minutes to come out and stating that if they refused to obey, the house would be set on fire.

The ultimatum was ignored. The fight went on.

After some time a policeman managed to climb to a corner of the roof where he could not be attacked by the defenders, and he set fire to the thatch. Soon the roof was one mass of flames. The position of the defenders became untenable.

At last the kitchen door was opened from the inside. Seven men came out, snorting and coughing. The last to emerge was Neil McGilligan. His face was blacked, his hair was singed, and there was a look of wild, mad hate and despair in his eyes.

He was no sooner outside than he was arrested and marched away handcuffed. The people of Glenmore stood around with despair and sorrow stamped on their faces, and they watched the prisoner being led away and, at the same time, the roof-tree of their ancient *Cúirt* falling in amid showers of sparks and spurts of flame.

But more was to come. The rule of law would have to prevail. The alternative was anarchy. This nest of sedition and rebellion would have to be destroyed.

Accordingly, the battering-ram was brought into action and the two end-walls were knocked in. This was surely the end of *Cúirt na hÉigse*.

Three months in jail Neil McGilligan got for resisting the officers of the law and leading an assault on them while they were 'in discharge of their lawful duty'.

Three long weary months without a scrap of news from home, and the home of his fathers destroyed forever. And, in the meantime, his wife and his little ones! He had hopes that they would not be left out to starve on the roadside. Here his confidence was not misplaced. His family were given food and shelter while he was absent.

At last his release came and he set out on his homeward journey. As he approached the Rosses bonfires blazed on the hill-sides to welcome him. But his greatest and most pleasant surprise awaited him. When he arrived back in the Glen he found his ancestral home re-built, re-roofed, and thatched more securely than ever.

There was no doubt about it, *Cúirt na hÉigse* was indestructible. 'Tara was grass', but the *Cúirt* would endure to the end of time!

III

On his way from Glasgow Black Jimmy Boyle was thinking of the history of Glenmore. There was no one left in the Glen now. The last families had left seven years before that. He knew that much from reports reaching him from time to time. It would be a dreary home-coming. But he would visit old scenes and recall old friends. He would stand on the top of Diarach and look at the mountains and the sea and the islands. And, of course, he would visit his native Glenmore. He would walk every step of it, visit every ruin in it, right down to *Cúirt na hÉigse.*

These reflections set him thinking of the last of the McGilligans – Cathal. He left the Glen some years after I left it myself, thought Jimmy. He wrote me a few letters from America. Then he stopped. How I'd love to have him with me for the few days I am to spend in the Rosses.

His laugh, I believe, would banish my sadness. Often I imagine I see him, hear him. The glint in his eye, his hearty laugh, his sense of humour, and his inimitable stories!

Black Jimmy came to the Rosses and put up in the house of a relative in the village of Cloghansalach. ('The town' they called it').

The village and the surrounding districts were in the fever of an election campaign. A meeting was to be held on the following day – Sunday – and the most prominent of the nation's leaders was billed to speak at it.

Hundreds had come into the village from the surrounding districts. The local fife and drum band was out in all its splendour. Flags flew from almost every window.

Black Jimmy strolled down to the meeting. It was presided over by a local publican … He felt honoured, he said, by being allowed to introduce to the people of the Rosses, one of Ireland's greatest statesmen and patriots.

The speaker got to his feet. There was a tremendous burst of applause. He stood there as if he enjoyed it until it had died down like the last mumbling echoes of a thunder clap. Then he began. His party, he said, wanted five years more. At the end of that time the Nation would be so solidly based that even a government of their opponents could not shake it. They had a five-year plan for the economic and cultural regeneration of the country. Along with providing employment for everybody they would see to it that the Irish language became once again the vernacular of the nation. They would save the *Gaeltacht*, because the *Gaeltacht* was the life and soul of the language, as the language was the life and soul of the nation!

At this point Black Jimmy Boyle left the meeting.

The following day he made his way to his native Glenmore. At the head of the Glen he stood on a height and looked at the roofless houses, right down to the sea.

He went down by the side of the river. When he was in the middle of the Glen he sighted the gaping walls of the old schoolhouse. As he approached the ruin he saw a picture in his mind's eye. A young woman coming to the school on a morning in early summer. She is leading her eldest child by the hand – a boy of five years. They reached the school. The woman knocked at the door and the two walk in. It was a strange family; a houseful of children and no mother. A serene-looking, elderly man said something to the woman – asked her a question, evidently. 'James Boyle', answered the woman. The man took a large book from a press and opened it out on the table. Wrote something in it. Asked more questions. Made further entries in the big book … The mother left, after telling the child she would be back for him in a few hours. For those few hours he was sad and lonely. Afterwards he found out that his mother was equally sad and lonely at home.

Black Jimmy recalled the later years of his school life. The maps on the walls, the rickety, old desks, the piece of board over the doorway with the words 'Glenmore National School' crudely printed on it. When Black Jimmy came back to have a look at the old ruin, the board with its crude lettering and English placename was no longer over the doorway. Long years before that it was taken down and replaced by a solid plaque of Rosses granite with the words '*Scoil Náisiúnta an Ghleanna Mhóir*' neatly cut in it.

Jimmy went along down to the ruins of the *Cúirt*. The fireplace end of the kitchen was crumbling. The skew-stone had fallen out of the chimney breast and lay on the hearth with a corner chipped off. Nettles and other weeds were growing on the floor along the walls where dust and then seeds had been blown in by the wind. The window sills were soiled and stained from the droppings of seafowl that had come into the ruin for shelter in the storm.

Black Jimmy looked out at the sea and across the bay to Illanala. Not one family on the island now. In his young days there were thirty five.

Jimmy thought of the night he brought Cathal McGilligan to the island wounded in the shoulder. It was rather stormy. 'I was dreadfully afraid crossing the Bar', said he in his own mind … 'I wonder is Cathal still alive. What would I not give for one hour with him! His laugh would make me young again'.

IV

Black Jimmy heard someone clearing his throat outside. Then the figure of a man appeared in the doorway.

'Black Jimmy Boyle?' he asked in a pronounced American accent.

'That is what they called me long ago. But you have the advantage over me. I don't know you'.

'I suppose you don't. I wouldn't know you either only I knew you had come. I was told yesterday evening. I got on your traces this morning. Heard you had left for the Glen. And here we are'.

'But, in heaven's name, who are you?'

'And so you don't know Cathal McGilligan?'

'Cathal!'

'Where are you staying?' asked Jimmy.

'With relations of my mother's in Ardglass. The young school-master there has lent me his car. I can't tell you how delighted I am to find you here. We'll have a great week together. That's all the time I have left ... I spent a few minutes at an election meeting yesterday. Marvellous conversions to the cause of Ireland, a nation'.

'We must visit Illanala', he continued.

'There is nobody living on the island now. All gone. But we must visit it. Are you as good a helmsman now as you were the night you took me across over forty years ago?'

'Hardly', replied Black Jimmy. 'And I was afraid that night. I should, of course, have looked for a big boat and a crew. But time was pressing'.

'I was afraid myself too', said Cathal. 'When she shipped two or three heavy seas in the Bar, I thought our last hour had come'.

'But you kept on singing'.

'It was all I could do. Sitting there strapped up in bandages. But I tell you I was afraid. The only one of the three of us who wasn't afraid was the little dark-eyed nurse from Ballyshannon. She was one great girl. Her musical lilt and her burst of fairy laughter still ring in my ears'.

'I wonder is she still alive?'

'Alive and hale and hearty. In New York, with her grandchildren around her. She went to America in the early twenties. Could get no post at home. Later on she married a teacher from the County Derry who had been dismissed for refusing to take the Oath of Allegiance. (An oath hadn't become an empty formula at the time) ... I spent two days in her house last summer. She sang some of the old songs for me. In an ageing voice. But my imagination helped me … She was asking for you. By the way, Jimmy, had you a spasm on her? Didn't you meet her a few times after the week we spent in Illanala?'

'I saw her once, one little while and then no more', quoted Black Jimmy in a somewhat sad voice.

'However, we must visit the island', went on Cathal. 'We'll get a boat in Bunbeg'.

The following day the two exiles were rowed across to Illanala by a Magheralosk fisherman. They proceeded to walk through the island.

'This is the house where I stayed long ago', commented Cathal as they stood before the ruins of what had once been a fine country house. Portion of the fireplace end had fallen in. On a lawn overgrown with weeds in front of the ruin lay the skeleton of an old boat. Beside the window there was a rusty pot and, almost covered with long grass, the rotted remains of a child's boat.

They went along to the old school-house. The windows were broken. There were several holes in the roof. The door was still kept shut by a heavy, rusted padlock. And, over the doorway, there was a solid plaque of granite with the words *Scoil Náisiúnta Oileán Eala* engraved on it.

'I remember when it was Illanala National School', said Black Jimmy. 'The average yearly attendance was over fifty. Now it is *Scoil Náisiúnta Oileán Eala*. And just look at it'.

'It is a consolation to reflect that it was rebaptised in the Gaelic faith before it was deserted and abandoned to the elements', remarked Cathal.

The next place they decided to visit was the Commeen Glen. When they came as far as the little bridge, Cathal stopped the car.

'Got a terrible shock there one day long ago', as if speaking to himself. 'I thought my brain had snapped. I was on the verge of collapse. For a few seconds I was ready to throw up everything. But I recovered'.

Cathal did not explain or amplify. Black Jimmy asked no questions. The car was started again and they drove on. Away along miles of a winding road through bleak bogland. Beyond Abhainn na Marbh they stopped again. A few hundred yards from the road stood the remains of a dwelling-house and outhouses. The little patches of land that had once been tilled were now waterlogged and overgrown with rushes. At the gable-end of the house there was a solitary rowan tree, bent away from the north-west wind.

'The poor Beezer, that is where he played when he was a boy. Down there in the stream he fished for minnows. In that little field one harvest day he threw down his reaping hook – like Cathal More of the Wine-Red Hand – and went off with the Column. They captured him outside Churchill as he lay bleeding in the bed of a dry stream. And they finished him off'.

They started off again. Down the Corkscrews and eastwards along the glen in the direction of Loughbarra.

'Nothing but ruins everywhere', remarked Cathal as they stopped again – this time in Upper Commeen. 'You remember the brown-haired, young woman who lived there with her husband and her three little children. She would get up at any hour of the night and leave her bed to two or three of us. She would share the bread of her children with us. And her man would put on an old frieze overcoat and go up to the top of the height. He would sit there in the shelter of a rock, ready to give the alarm if he saw a light blinking anywhere from the Gap of Glendowan to Doochary Bridge ... Ah, the plain people of Ireland! The poor people! They gave all they had – for a dream. A pleasant dream, some would say. Others would call it a nightmare. In any case, they woke up in the cold, grey dawn. They walked out with their children, without bothering to lock their doors, and they made their way to the nearest town. They were the 'wild geese' of their day. But their flight will never be recorded in song or story'.

Two or three days afterwards they were back again at the ruins of the *Cúirt* in Glenmore.

'It was subject to fierce attacks in its day', began Cathal. 'First, the Night of the Big Wind. But it was rebuilt. Then over half a century afterwards came the landlords with their armed policemen. They sent the roof up in flames and battered down portions of the walls. But that did not finish it. Then came the third attack – in the days of the Black and Tans. You remember it. A few days after the Crolly ambush a British gunboat appeared in Aran roads. Thousands of soldiers were landed at Burtonport and, in a few hours, swarmed through the Rosses. Their agents had told them what points to attack. And, of course, the *Cúirt* was on the list. We knew that any attempt at resistance would be hopeless. So we all cleared out. I was hiding inside the mouth of a cave halfway up the Glen. I saw the roof going up in flames and lighting the surface of the sea all the way across to Illanala. Many people thought this was the end of the *Cúirt*, that it would never be rebuilt after the third time destroyed. But before six months it was fully renovated. It certainly did look as if it couldn't be destroyed. Then came the fourth attack – this time in the name of the Irish nation'.

'Tell me all about that attack', said Black Jimmy. 'As you know, I wasn't in the Glen at the time'.

'I know you were not. You were behind barbed wire. And it was my fault – to have sent you on such a mission. I did not have time to think that a new testing had become necessary. That a man who could not be intimidated could be purchased. So I sent you with a man who betrayed you. However, to go on with my story. As you see, the *Cúirt* here was built very close to the edge of the cliff. My father and another man he could trust had made a tunnel leading down to the caves. Well, a few of us were holding a meeting one night. We must have been given away for we weren't half an hour in the house when the place was surrounded by the Staters. They knocked at the door. No reply. They knocked again and again. No reply. At last they burst the door open and rushed in. They searched but found nobody. And, of course, they did not find the entrance to the tunnel. They never dreamt it was beneath the hearth-stone of an innocent-looking fireplace in one of the bedrooms.

'Well, they were mad. They thought that we had got wind of the raid and that we had escaped by sea in the darkness. So they decided to make it impossible for us to meet here anymore. They set the house on fire. In the morning there was nothing left of the *Cúirt* but blackened, gaping walls.

'It was surely destroyed this time … But it was not. After the Civil War it was reroofed – for the fourth time. And many people were beginning to believe that it could not be destroyed. Tara was grass. The Castle in Donegal was a heap of crumbling ruins. Of the Four Masters' Abbey, nothing was left but a few broken arches. They had all been destroyed by the brute force of the foreigners. But brute force, whether exercised by the foreigner or by the native, could not put an end to the *Cúirt* of Glenmore'.

'Yet look at it now!'

'You must have been heart-broken leaving it?' said Black Jimmy.

'I was, indeed. It was heart-breaking to see the *Cúirt* coming to an end. If it hadn't been for that, it would not have been half as difficult to leave. I would have left when the worship of the Golden Calf had become nationwide, but I wanted the *Cúirt* to continue. I was married and had two children. And I fondly hoped that my little boy would take my place after I was gone. Then came two bad seasons. The crops failed. There was no worthwhile fishing. The people of the Glen began to leave. They would all go in a short space of time. I knew I could not live in the Glen without neighbours. So, one fine morning, Fanny and myself and the two kids walked out. We arrived in Belfast that evening, crossed to Liverpool the following day. Three years after that, when we had saved our passage money, we went to America. That's quite a lot about myself. And I've never asked you how you got on in life or who you are married to'.

'To a girl from the County Mayo that I got to know in Glasgow', replied Black Jimmy. 'I was getting on a bit when I got married. This girl's family had gone through hard times. Their home was burned by the British. Afterwards it was wrecked by the Staters. Their most trying time came after 1932. They were being harassed night and day by detectives. In the end they cleared out'.

'We have only one more day', said Cathal in a sad tone of voice. 'I must leave for Dublin on Wednesday morning to get the plane for New York that evening. Any particular place you want to go?'

'I'd like to go to Kincasslagh to visit Plunkett O'Boyle's grave'.

'I too want to go', said Cathal. 'Poor Plunkett. Like the Beezer he was shot dead and he an unarmed prisoner. But unlike the Beezer, Plunkett was slaughtered by his own countrymen. I will certainly visit his grave. And there is another grave I must visit – my grandmother's grave in Cruit.

They went to Kincasslagh. Later on they went to the old graveyard in Cruit. They knelt down on a grave and each said a prayer. Then Cathal picked up a little pebble and put it in an envelope. He put the envelope in his pocket. 'When I go back home', he said, 'I'll have this little pebble set, and leave it to my children, to pass on to their children'. Then he stood up and faced his companion.

'Poor granny!' he said, in a sad voice. 'If I had heeded her dying words, while they could not have prevented my defeat, they would have saved me from bitter disappointment. I'd have been prepared for what was coming. She had her moment of inspiration and we thought it was delirium. 'Tell him', she said, 'not to expect too much. For the day would come when some of the leading warriors of the Craobhruadh[3] will go over to the sons of Cailitín, and they will divide the spoils between them'. That day came in 1922. It was bad, as you know. But it was nothing compared to what took place ten years afterwards. The second defection was miles worse than the first, because it was led by those who had advocated and taken part in the armed resistance against the first betrayal. And to crown all they have the brazen effrontery to say that Ireland is free, and that they freed her'.

Later on in the evening they drove to Cloghansalach, where Black Jimmy Boyle was staying. 'It's early yet', said Cathal looking at his watch. 'We'll walk slowly up to the top of Knockfree and have one more look at the Rosses'.

They reached the top of the height and sat down on two boulders. They looked around them in all directions. Black Jimmy was the first to break the silence. 'We are nearly as lonely as Donnchadh Scaite[4] was the first day he came into the Rosses'.

'In a way we are worse', replied Cathal. 'Whatever grievance Donnchadh may have had against Little Dark Agnes, he had no cruel memories of the Rosses'.

Later on they came down to the village where Cathal had left the car. There they stood and looked at each other. Black Jimmy wanted to ask his companion a final question.

'Have you any hope left for Ireland?' he asked.

'I wouldn't say I am entirely without hope', replied Cathal. 'Eight centuries is a long time for national aspirations to survive at all. Hard to think they will die now'.

'But have you any hope for the present generation?'

'None whatsoever. Nor much for the next. Some people will tell you that there are grunts and protests already. But the grunts and protests, for the most part, are coming from people whose grievance is that they are not getting a better deal in power and privilege and patronage. Just like one of a gang of robbers who thinks he hasn't got a fair share of the swag. So I don't expect any genuine regeneration for a long time to come yet. We are going through a terrible nightmare – a combination of coercion and corruption. Still, I have a ray of hope that it won't last forever … And now', he concluded, 'I must be going. I have to leave this friendly lad back his car, and I have to collect a few things for the morning'.

He held out his hand. Black Jimmy grasped it but did not speak. For a few seconds they looked at each other in silence.

'Good-bye, Jimmy', Cathal managed to say.

'Aren't you glad we've had this week together?'

No answer.

'Speak, man', said Cathal. 'Aren't you glad we've had this week together?'

'I- I- am. I am. I am, Cathal', said Black Jimmy Boyle.

And they parted.

Notes
1   I am unable to locate any Gaelic version of this story.
2   Some of the details in this story refer to the history of Séamus Ó Grianna's native Rannafast. Séamus was descended from a long line of poets and Aodh, Séamus and Peadar were three of the most famous of them.
3   The Knights of the Red Branch. This refers to the Ulster Branch of Gaelic literature where Cú Chulainn stars.
4   A half-brother of Red Hugh O'Donnell.

IRISH ARTISTS[1]
(A Reply to Peadar O'Donnell)[2]

Those of us who have written something in Irish found Peadar O'Donnell's article on 'Irish Artists' which appeared in last week's *An Phoblacht* very interesting. I found it particularly so as I had given up hope where Gaelic writing is concerned and was actually about to attempt an English translation of my book of short stories for publication in America.

I agree with all that Peadar O'Donnell says about translation, only that I would remind him of what Robbie Burns said to the 'glaikit, gleesome, dainty damies' who came from 'Castalia's wimplin' streamies'[3] to reprimand the smuggler who took a job as a gauger. Apart from this consideration – and perhaps the reason why he didn't stress it was because he thought it too obvious – he has said the truth about translation.

But Peadar seems very hopeful when he writes about the future that is before Gaelic writers. I think a little explanation will make him modify his opinion on the matter. When a man like Peadar O'Donnell gives serious thought to Gaelic culture and Gaelic literature, the least thing we might do is to inform him fully as to the present position. So, to make matters clear beyond doubt I will take a concrete example.

Peadar O'Donnell and I have each of us written a book on the life of the Rosses folk, and people who have read and understood the two books found a certain resemblance between them in almost every chapter. I mean *Islanders*[4] and *Caisleáin Óir*.[5] Now to make the position clear to Peadar I will ask him to suppose the case reversed and tell me if he would have any hope in the future of English fiction. Suppose that English was spoken only where Irish is spoken at present – the *Gaeltacht* – and that Irish was the language of the rest of Ireland. That Irish was the language of the legislature and of practically every branch of the administration. That Irish was the language of England and of England's Empire, and also of the United States. That at home the English speakers, living on kelp and carrigeen along the narrow strip of bogs and boulders from Dingle to the Rosses were too poor to buy *Islanders*. That the only sale for it in Ireland was in schools and colleges. That those who read it could never get near, say, the death of Mrs. Doogan, that they were around her deathbed with notebooks to get the last subjunctive mood or irregular verb from her before she died. And suppose they got certificates and degrees for their collections of subjunctives from inspectors who were equally dead to the realities of Gaelic literature. Imagine all that, Peadar, and you will have a kind of idea of how the writer who makes Irish his medium is situated.

When Peadar O'Donnell writes a book some people will disagree violently with him. Others will express their warmest appreciation of him. It doesn't matter (for the purposes of this argument) whom he provokes. His stories are read as human records, not as collections of grammar or idioms.

The Gaelic Revival movement was at its best only a linguistic movement. It was never a literary movement or anything approaching it. It never made any appeal to those who wanted to write. The few who chose Irish as their literary medium did so for the best reason possible – because it was their native language and the only language that could express the life they knew and could write about.

That is all I have to say for the present except that I hope to see more from Peadar on the subject.

Notes

1   *An Phoblacht*, 2.7.32, 6.
2   He was a lifelong friend of Séamus Ó Grianna. He was a teacher, writer, editor, revolutionary, Republican, socialist. See, Robert Welch (ed.), *The Oxford Companion to Irish Literature* (OUP, 1996) 422-3.
3   From *Epistle to Dr. Blacklock: In answer to a letter*.
4   1929.
5   1924.

PLIGHT OF IRISH ARTISTS[1]
A Letter from 'Máire'

To the Editor:

Sir,

In his short article in a recent issue of *An Phoblacht*[2] Peadar O'Donnell in one sentence gets down to some bedrock principles of Gaelic Literature. 'I feel even in myself', he says, 'the need for the Gaelic idiom to voice aspects of the life of Ireland of today'. Those who do not understand the *Gaeltacht* and who have read the superb descriptions in *Islanders*[3] and *Adrigoole*[4] will find it hard to believe that Peadar feels the need for any medium other than the one he has so far used in his writings. But I can easily believe him because I know the types of Rosses characters which he has put into his books. And I am sure he must have often felt sorry to translate *Murchadh Antoin Chathaoir* and *Séamas a' Ghleanna* and the rest of them.

The *Gaeltacht* is still with us. It is a living reality. It is as different from the rest of Ireland as France is from England. The people of the *Gaeltacht* speak Irish to express their ideals, not to show that they know this relative form or that subjunctive mood. Therefore, there is material, living material, for literature in the *Gaeltacht*. Outside the *Gaeltacht* there is only material for grammar and a little philology. In the *Gaeltacht* we express our joys and our sorrows in Irish. Outside the *Gaeltacht* we talk about the Indo-Germanic *V* and the Glottal Stop. Need I ask which of the two forms a basis for literature?

I could not write in Irish about Dublin life, even if I tried it.[5] And the reason is because there is no life in Dublin of which Irish is the expression. For the same reason I could not write in English about my native *Rann na Feirste*. I might give awkward translations of *Eoin Rua* or *Condaí Éamainn* but their own mothers wouldn't know them in the new garb.

Binn Blasta – Rubbish!

As I said in a recent article, I wrote in Irish because it is the only language that could adequately describe the life and the people I knew. I did not use Irish as a medium because it was the language of *Pádraig, Bríd* and *Colm Cille* or because it is a *teanga bhinn bhlasta*. I detest all that rubbish as does almost everybody from the *Gaeltacht*. The *binn blasta, Pádraig, Bríd* mentality was and is like a *crann smola* hanging over the Gaelic writer. No native thought, no creative talent could grow or develop under its blighting influence. I know it was useful as propaganda, perhaps necessary. But propaganda chokes art as weeds could choke one of the open drains we have in the Rosses.

Peadar O'Donnell says we must get back to original work. And, of course, we must if we are to help to build a modern native literature. But how are we going to tackle the problem? I am writing Irish for exactly twenty years. Of that period I have spent eighteen years at original work (in one form or another) and two years at translation. In 1928 I had published four original books. In 1929 I wrote what I consider by far my best work – *Inis Beannach*. What happened it? Where is it? Lying under a heap of dust in the company of tailors' bills and income tax demands. That is my answer to anyone who asks me why I gave up original work and took to translation. I couldn't get a publisher for my novel (unless I gave it away for practically nothing).

That *Gúm* Again!

Why didn't I submit *Inis Beannach* to the *Gúm, arsa tusa*. Well, I didn't. I looked on the *Gúm* as a friend of mine estimated a new patent razor he had bought. 'It is very handy', said he. It pares my nails and sharpens my pencil and cuts my tobacco. It will do everything but shave'. Well, my opinion of this literary department was that it could do something with everything except literature. So I didn't tax it beyond its capacity. Now I don't blame men for having being born without any literary feeling. Nor would I be too harsh on the Civil Servants (or was it the typewriters) that mutilated Seosamh Mac Grianna's magnificent *Eoghan Ruadh Ó Néill*. I am sure Seosamh must have often heard his father telling about the Rosses *lúircíneach* that risked getting a few broken ribs to be able afterwards to say '*Bhí mé ag troid le Micheál Dhónaill Ruaidh*'. Well, when men are made literary judges on account of their political allegiance, it is only natural that, realising the insecurity of political backing, they would want to be in a position to say: 'We corrected *Eoghan Ruadh Ó Néill*. It is a good book, Mr. Minister, but we had to trim it for him'.

Some Difficulties

Peadar O'Donnell wants us to point out our difficulties and to propose a solution of those difficulties. Well, while I can see the difficulties plainly, I cannot see the solution under the circumstances. But perhaps someone else would propose something that would enable Gaelic writers to go on with original work and keep outside the walls of the workhouse at the same time. So here are some of the difficulties.

1 We have only a very limited reading public. And for the most part those who could understand us do not read us and those who read us do not understand it.

2 We have novelists trying to write schoolbooks and newspaper articles (to live) and school masters and journalists trying to write novels.

3 We have against us all the vested interests that have grown or are supposed to have grown out of the language movement.

4 We have congenital idiocy in university robes mumbling inanities about Gaelic literature and Gaelic scholarship.

5 We have men writing about Gaelic folklore who couldn't converse for five minutes with a *Gaeltacht seanchaí*.

6 We have the *Gúm* novelist writing 'books' with Dinneen's dictionary at the one elbow and O'Neill Lane on the other.

7 We have opposed to us 90% of the thousands who have a smattering of Irish.

8 We lost the Battle of Kinsale.

9 And found *Rowdalam Randy* and *Crooka Glass na h-Erin* and *Dornán Dán*.

10 There is an organised boycott against our books by what Carlyle would call hod-bearers who want to be architects and who were born for hod-bearing.

11 Our native knowledge of Irish and any original work we produce are positive hindrances to us in our struggle for existence. Why wouldn't Seosamh Mac Grianna or Donn Piatt or Niall Ó Dónaill be appointed professor of Irish literature in one of the university colleges? Why? Well, there would be contrasts. And the 'hod-bearers

might be reduced to hod-bearing' if an architect came on the scene.

Two Forms of Censorship

Donn Piatt has something to say about censorship. It is quite true that you cannot censor an atmosphere, but there would be no necessity to censure the literature of the *Gaeltacht*. I couldn't conceive myself or Donn or Seosamh or any of the Gaelic writers that I know writing anything that would need to be censored. Of course there are two kinds of censorship. There is the censorship by the Civil Servant whose idea of efficiency is a page of blue pencil marks. And there is the censorship which is by some considered necessary for the sake of morality or decency or both. I will never submit to the former brand of censorship unless indeed I am very hungry and they find it out and try to humiliate me. But as for censorship on grounds of public morality and decency, I will always submit to the censorship of the Gael – of the Catholic Gael with fifteen centuries of tradition behind him in faith and nationality. But let me be understood in the original. Let no man try to get the meaning of Irish, the full meaning and weight and colour, let no man try to get it in translation. There is where the danger lies. I remember the Gaelic League Executive bringing me to book once for quoting two oft-quoted lines in the official organ of the League:

Dá dtagaidís na feara-choin a bhí tamall uainn sa Spáinn
Dá dtagaidís do chacfaidís ar lucht na bheistí bán.

For centuries these lines were quoted by the Gael in times of national stress. But the members of the Gaelic League Executive translated it and found it vulgar.

What Can We Do?

And now, what are we going to do? The case is very urgent. The *Gaeltacht* is dying, dying fast. This generation will finish it. And with the *Gaeltacht* goes all the hope of a Gaelic literature. Who will save it? Who will help to save it? It is perhaps something to know that we have the good will of Irishmen who write in English. There are certain things that these writers could do for us. They could make common cause with us and stand with us when we state the fundamental difference between a string of conjugations and declensions written by a B.A. in Celtic Studies, and a story written in Gaelic by a Gael to be read by Gaels as a picture of human life in what remains of the Irish nation.

MÁIRE

Notes

1   *An Phoblacht*, 6.8.32, 7.
2   23.7.32, 6.
3   1928.
4   1929.
5   See, also, by Máire: 'Mé Féin is Baile Átha Cliath' which appeared in *The Irish Press* (14.2.51, 2).

How to Make Ireland Irish-Speaking[1]

In this age of greed and materialism and pessimism, it seems a thankless and a well-nigh hopeless task to offer any serious suggestions for the restoration of our Gaelic tongue. The materialist will say to you, what good is Irish to the masses and, sure, we cannot all be Cabinet Ministers or Chief Executive Officers or Chief Translators or Parliamentary Secretaries. The pessimist will tell you that it is impossible to revive it; that the position with regard to Irish is much worse today than it was forty years ago after all our Gaelic League resolutions, Compulsory Irish in the University, Bilingual Programmes, Summer Courses and Degrees in Celtic Studies. To the materialist, however, I would say that nations have souls, and, to the pessimist I would say: 'Thou of little faith'. The Irish language is our national inheritance although it may be dead at the moment. But, with faith and determination, we can bring it back to life again.

I have given this matter quite a lot of time and thought and the scheme I am going to propose is the outcome of years of patient thinking and study, spurred on by the desire to see *Éire arís ag Cáit Ní Dhuibhir*. I am quite conscious of the fact that this scheme of mine has its imperfections. But, with all its shortcomings, it is vastly superior to all the other schemes and criticisms that we get from time to time. And its superiority lies in the fact that it is a constructive scheme. I do not tell how to destroy. I show how to build. Any fool can reduce a mansion to ruins but it takes an architect to build one. I have thought out a scheme for the revival of Irish that will be at the same time practical and in keeping with the national dignity. And, if any man accuses me of having a selfish motive in putting forward these suggestions, I can easily silence him by telling him that I am not eligible for appointment under any of my proposed schemes as I happen to be a native speaker.

When I speak of reviving the Irish language I mean making it the spoken language of Ireland as English is at present (outside the *Gaeltacht*), or as French is in France, or Italian in Italy. I know that it will be a very difficult task to revive a dead language. At first sight it seems impossible. It seems that a language once dead is dead forever. That it obeys the laws of nature like everything that has life. The fallacy of this argument lies in the assumption that the principle of life in a language is the same as that of a human being or other animal. I know several people in Dublin who have brought Irish back from the dead and speak it fluently. I grant you that it smells of charnel house, but only to the people of the *Gaeltacht*. And these constitute so small a fraction of the nation that we can afford to ignore them. (Anyway, why didn't they accept the Cromwellian alternative to Connaught and not be bothering us when we are engaged in a work of national importance?) It can be proved beyond the shadow of a doubt that Irish can be revived. And, if in the past our efforts were not successful, it is largely because we did not work on proper lines.

The first thing we must do is to abolish all existing organizations. Let no man talk to me of reform. Reform is not revolution, and revolution is the only thing that can make Ireland Irish-speaking. Hence I say scrap all existing organizations and establish a new organization, the object of which shall be to restore the ancient tongue of the Gael to the proud position it once occupied. I will not give this organization any name for the present. It will not be difficult to get a name for it. I think the geniuses that have given us Lána Tone for Tone's Lane, and Cumann na Daraíochta for Dairying Association can be safely entrusted with the task of giving our new organization a suitable name.

I will now assume that the organization is established and that I myself am a member of it. (The fact that the scheme is entirely of my own creation ought to outweigh all prejudices against me as a native speaker). Then our first task will be to draw up a set of rules, or a constitution, if you will. I do not foresee any great difficulty in this part of our work. The difficulties will not arise until we try to interpret the constitution. But even then we can easily solve all our problems under that heading by having a few men on our Executive Council who will see to it that the proper interpretation is put on every clause and section and subsection.

We will have branches of our organization throughout the country, a Central Executive Committee, and an annual *Ard-Fheis*. The selection of members for the Central Executive will be a very important thing. And I propose here, without apology to anyone, that there should be one test and one test only, namely, the candidates' fitness for membership. Let no man be elected to the Central Executive Committee unless he has a firm grip on fundamentals. We must take a lesson from the failure of the organizations which we intend to abolish, and make sure that we elect only men who will insist on differentiating between *leasrún* and *aguisín*. It seems superfluous to insist on this qualification. But we must at all cost avoid the mistakes of the past. I have seen very large assemblies convened to consider grave language questions, and try to find a solution for them, and after three hours debating they were unable to decide whether a particular motion was a *leasrún* or an *aguisín*. Time and again I have seen them disperse and no one seemed to know whether it was a *leasrún* or an *aguisín*. I do not like to say bitter things but I find it very hard to banish from my heart all feelings of bitterness against men who imagined they could revive a language without first making clear the fundamental difference between *leasrún* and *aguisín*.

But in this organization which, with the goodwill and assistance of the people of Ireland, I propose to establish, we pledge ourselves never to leave the Council chamber until we explore every avenue to prevent an *aguisín* masquerading in the old guise of a *leasrún* and vice versa. And when we have that satisfactorily settled we must get down to our work in real earnest. I can mention here only a few of the things that require the prompt and special attention of the Executive Committee. The ancient name of Kingston is Dún Laoghaire and a Dublin daily insists on calling it Kingston. We must get after that paper and point out to it that we owe allegiance to no king. *Agus mura nglaca sé comhairle, glacadh sé comhrac*. If it does not take heed and mend its manners we will pass a resolution condemning it for its unpatriotic practice. We must then turn our attention to the schools. It is a well-know fact that several schools have the name engraven in English on the stone over the doorway. We must insist on having the name in Irish on every school, or where Irish only is not practicable we must see that it shall be in Irish side by side with English. Then there are other crying abuses which touch on fundamental issues in the revival of Irish as a spoken language. For example, names of railway stations, public signposts, English income tax forms and evictions in the *Gaeltacht* by non-Irish-speaking bailiffs.

Our new organization will be strictly non-political. Of late years there has been a lot of confusion on this point, so much so that I believe it is my duty to explain it fully and avoid misunderstandings in future. No member of the organization can take part in politics as a member of the organization. On this point clearness is absolutely necessary. And I will give an illustration of what I mean. Say Liam Shylock is a member of the organization. To make the point clear beyond doubt, suppose he is the president. Now Liam can take part in politics and even aspire to parliamentary honours and emoluments, but on no account can the president have any part in politics. That would be against the fundamentals of our constitution.

I foresee some difficulties in our way here. For, since our aim is to make Irish the spoken language of Ireland, and since that end cannot be achieved unless it is made a government policy, it may happen that we should find ourselves called upon to attack or defend the government in power according as we think it will serve our interests. We must be very careful in our attitude towards governments. If we could be sure of having the same government in office for a generation we could adopt a settled policy. But, from time to time, the old order changeth and when such changes occur, it is very important to get some of our men into key positions. Hence when an attack on an existing government is the order of the day, I would make this suggestion: try to get unanimous resolution and don't let the Press get hold of the names of the proposer and seconder. Then the resolution will be put down to the entire organization and it will not be remembered against any individual member if and when the change comes. But an individual member may profitably attack a government on its language policy immediately after it has gone out of office. This plan is not without its dangers as the outgoing political party may return again to power. At this stage no hard and fast rules can be laid down. Neither can I say that it is a matter for individual judgment and discretion. It is a matter of instinct. And no-one should attempt it except those whose instincts guided them in the past to abandon lost causes at the right time. The same unerring instinct will also guide them to espouse winning causes at the right time.

The language of the Executive Committee shall be Irish. And no one will be admitted as a member unless he can make a speech. In order to help members to fulfil their functions successfully, I propose that a handbook be published containing, among other things, at least seven proverbs, for example: *ní túisce deoch ná scéal*. Then, if we want a classical flavour, we can easily get a list of Latin phrases at the end of any good English dictionary. An occasional French phrase too would give our assembly a bit of tone. That should not be very difficult to procure. Most of us have spent a weekend in Paris or have been to Lourdes on a pilgrimage, or have a gramophone or Senior Honours in Intermediate French.

We must be prepared to face every difficulty we meet with, no matter how formidable it may appear. It is surprising how difficulties which stagger one at first sight can be overcome when they are met with determination. Hence we will not shirk any task no matter how enormous it may appear. When a question arises that requires serious thought and prompt action, a special meeting of the Central Executive, having given the matter full and deliberate consideration, will appoint a sub-committee of experts to go into the matter and report on it. If the Executive consider the matter beyond the scope of its jurisdiction it can put it on the agenda for the *Ard-Fheis*. And the *Ard-Fheis*, being the supreme authority on all matters concerning the organization, can refer it back to the Central Executive Committee which in its turn will have power under the constitution to appoint a sub-committee to deal with it. This mode of procedure will make for peace and harmony in the organization without which the language couldn't make much progress.

We must pay special attention to the schools and colleges, including the university. Up to the present Irish has not had its rightful place in our Educational Programmes. There was little or no attempt made to make Irish the spoken language of the school. Not one in a thousand school children today can give you the Irish for Duplicate Ration or Economic Solution or Metaphysical Entity or Fourth Dimensional, or anything that would tend to restore Irish as the vernacular of this nation. Hence, realizing the important part played by the schools and colleges, we will revolutionise the entire system of education from top to bottom. At present the things that would lead to the re-Gaelicising of Ireland are being sadly neglected, mainly because the teachers are not qualified to teach the language. It is impossible within the compass of this short article to state the requirements of a good professor of Irish. But I will mention a few of the essential qualifications which we should insist on in professors of Irish, always bearing in mind that our object is to revive Irish as the everyday language of the nation.

A professor of Irish should know all about *opjareois*. For example, that the initial vowel is sometimes suppressed in small proclitic words, such as *con tein* for *ocon tein*. He should know that between vowels the Indo-German *v* is either dropped as in *dia*, gen. *de*, Sanskrit, *deva*, or vocalized as in *nue* new, Gothic *niujis*, Sanskrit *naxya*. He should know that metathesis is common to all Celtic languages, that *die-thracair* comes from *du-fu-thracair*, Sanskrit root *tark*, *tarkayati*, to imagine. He should know all about the T-Preterite, the S-Preterite, the Reduplicated Future and Reduplicated Second Future.

And he should know all that is to be known about the Glottal Stop and the Svarabhakti.

It is sometimes suggested by ignorant people that we ought to get as many of our professors as possible from the *Gaeltacht*. But where will you find a native of the *Gaeltacht* with the necessary qualifications? The ignorance of the native speaker in this respect is appalling. Some years ago I got a book on phonetics by a scholar of European reputation.[2] Ten pages were devoted to the Svarabhakti. The learned professor asserted that he found it in my native Rosses with one Pádraig Mac Conóglaigh. When I had read the book I went straight tro Pádraig whom I found sitting on a boulder outside his house mending the meshes of a lobster-pot. I confess that I should have considered *infra dig* to consult a man in his occupation on linguistic matters had not the learned philologist made special mention of him in his book.

'A Phádaí', arsa mise, 'an fíor go bhfuil Svarabhakti agat?'

'Damnú nár thige orm má bhí a leithéid d'acra agam ó chuir Dia mo cheann ar an tsaol', was the reply he made me. It is hard to believe it but there he was with a Svarabhakti and, not only did he not know anything about it, but he did not know that he had it at all.

I think I have said enough on this point to prove that in making Irish the spoken language of Ireland we can have no hope that we shall get any assistance from the *Gaeltacht*. In one way that will be to our advantage. If the *Gaeltacht* counted as a factor in re-Gaelicising the nation, we should, like our predecessors, be troubled with the *Gaeltacht* problem. We should have to call on the Government occasionally to give effect to the recommendations of the *Gaeltacht Commission* and pass other resolutions which would take up valuable time and tend to divert our attention from our main purpose –

making Irish the vernacular of this ancient and historic nation.

Notes

1   This article was first published in *An Gaedheal* Iml. 2 Uimh. 13, 30.3.35, 7 and Iml. 2 Uimh. 15, 13.4.35, 6.
2   Alf Sommerfelt, *The Dialect of Torr*, Co. Donegal (Christiania, 1922). This represents a study of the Gaelic dialect of an area in north-west Donegal near which Séamus had been a teacher for several years.

Compulsory Irish[1]

Sir,

I claim the right to say a few words on this all-important question. I claim it as one whose childhood's language was Irish and Irish only, and who went to a school where everything was taught through the medium of English. It was the same as what we have in the junior classes in the schools of the Twenty-six Counties today, with the position of the languages reversed, and with this difference: my teacher was a fluent speaker of English. I claim the right to speak as one who emigrated to an English-speaking country at the age of sixteen years; as a teacher who taught in different types of schools; as a parent who taught the language to every one of his children and succeeded in getting them to master it in spite of the Murder Machine of compulsory Irish.

Let there be no mistake about it, compulsion is killing what is left of the language. Therefore the man who is against compulsion is, whether he realizes it or not, the best friend of Irish. And he who supports compulsion is, whether he realizes it or not, the language's worst enemy.

Therefore I appeal to the parents to unite and make their voice heard in defence at once of their children and of our priceless heritage. I appeal to the teachers, many of whom understand the havoc that is being wrought by compulsion. Above all I appeal to our rulers to abolish compulsion before all is lost. I appeal to their patriotism, to their sense of justice, to their humanity. I will put one aspect of compulsory Irish before them, namely its result as it affects the *Gaeltacht*. I appeal to each and every one of them to ask himself in all sincerity before God is it right or just to compel the children of the *Gaeltacht* to spend four-fifths of their school life at Irish when they must emigrate afterwards to English-speaking countries to earn their living?

I do not suppose that this appeal of mine will be given much heed. I know that it will be heeded in years to come. I know that compulsion will and must be abolished. But by then it will be too late. All will be lost. Compulsion will have done its deadly work. However, I have the consolation of knowing that I have done my duty. I will die happy with the thought that I have made this last act of love and loyalty to the language that is and has been so near and dear to my heart.

Yours etc.,
Séamus Mac Grianna,
275 Griffith Avenue,
Dublin 9.

COMPULSORY IRISH[2]

Sir,

Since I wrote to your paper some days ago I have got scores of letters agreeing with me. Most of them said that the vast majority of the people of the State were against compulsion but that they were afraid to voice their opinion.

Now, I can understand a mother being afraid. Her children are being unmercifully hammered at school over Irish. She is afraid that they will get a worse hammering if she makes a public protest. I can understand the teacher who does not speak Irish at a teaching level trying to teach, say, arithmetic to children who do not understand Irish at any level. If he protests publicly he is afraid he will be victimized by the inspector. The inspector in turn is afraid of the man above him, or, as sometimes happens, has his eye on promotion.

I can understand such people being afraid and, to a certain extent, I sympathize with them. But I cannot understand the man or the woman who is afraid of being called by the 'fear gales' a shoneen or a West Briton or a slave. It is the only argument the racketeers have. And the more money they are making by supporting compulsory Irish the louder they hurl 'shoneen' and 'West Briton' and 'slave' at anyone who pleads for a realistic approach to the language and to sane methods of teaching it.

Some of us may have proved that we know Irish. We may have spent years teaching it. We may have considerable experience in the study of other living languages. But we are slaves if we oppose the compulsion racket. We are the product of centuries of oppression. Not so the champions of compulsory Irish, the 'True Gaels'. In some mysterious way, their ancestors came through the Dark Ages with lofty ideals and pure-souled patriotism. And so the glorious procession marches along, every member holding aloft in one hand a torch whose splendour (they maintain) had not been equalled in Ireland since her Golden Age of Saints and Scholars. The torch in one hand, and what about the other hand? The other hand is engaged in gathering in the shekels.

One gets used to being called a slave and a West Briton. In my native Donegal I have been called those names down through the years. Some of my traducers speak Irish, some not. Some others of them regarded Irish as mud before the Free State came into existence. They wanted to 'speak English and be dacint'. But some of the mud stuck and then came the day when it was worth gold.

But the people are at last beginning to shake off their torpor. The day will come when, with one voice, they will demand the abolition of compulsion. The Government in office will see clearly that compulsory Irish, far from being a political expedient, would do their party untold harm. Then they will put an end to it and the Minister will make the announcement in the Dáil. I can almost hear his speech ringing in my ears: 'Our efforts to revive Irish have ended in failure ... The attempt could never have succeeded at any time since the Great Famine ... We thought the people wanted Irish; that is why we kept up the effort. But the people do not want it, and we are here to obey the people's will ...'

And what will the racketeers do on that day? Will they raise one furious howl of protest that will resound from Malin Head to Cape Clear? Not on your life. They will immediately see that there is no future (for them) in opposing the will of a determined people. The most blatant and arrogant among them will be the first to acclaim the Government's decision and applaud the Minister's speech. They will, of course, get a bit of a jolt. But nothing to worry about. Only a temporary dislocation of activities. They will soon settle down again, and they will turn their undoubted talents to some other means of obtaining money under false pretences.

Yours etc.,
Séamus Mac Grianna,
275 Griffith Avenue, Dublin 9.

COMPULSORY IRISH[3]

Sir,

There are thousands upon thousands of people in this country who are opposed to the idea of trying to replace English by Irish as the vernacular of this nation. They think it could be done, but their objection to it is that it would keep us back for generations, which we cannot afford in this age of competition when we have far more pressing problems facing us than the replacement of one language by another. These people, not knowing Irish, do not know that it can never become the vernacular of the people. French, German, Spanish or Italian could, after centuries, replace English in this country if we were invaded and conquered by France, Germany, Spain or Italy. But Irish can never replace English as the vernacular of the Irish people.

And why not if English could be replaced by any one of the other languages I have mentioned? Because these other languages are fully flowered. Irish is an old language whose growth was arrested centuries ago. It was a beautiful language; even what remains of it is beautiful. For that reason, every assistance and encouragement should be given to anyone who wants to study it. But there is a world of difference between fostering a love of Irish and the attempt to make it, by brutal compulsion, the one and only language of the nation.

I have often asked myself what would happen if a law were passed that would allow nobody but a fluent speaker of Irish to become a member of our legislature. Let us say a parliament of native speakers to make sure of the fluency. The experiment would be worth a trial. It could indeed be the first step on the road from the emancipation of the country from the bondage of compulsory Irish. It would bring home to the masses that we are living in the second half of the twentieth century and not in the days of Cormac Mac Airt.

I can prove this point to the hilt. But, in doing so, I must begin by blowing what may seen to many people a blast on my own trumpet.

I am a very fluent speaker of Irish. I could go on talking for hours and hours, without once pausing to consider whether a noun was masculine or feminine, whether I should aspirate or not aspirate, whether I should use the conditional or subjunctive form of the verb. The language comes to me with the same ease and spontaneity as the drawing of my breath. It comes to me the way I want it - in gushes, in torrents, in squalls according to the theme I am speaking on. I can do all that any time I want to. And if I were a member of Dáil Éireann this very day I could do it - that is, if the Ceann Comhairle allowed me.

Why, someone will ask, wouldn't he? For the simple reason that he could not - provided, of course, he understood me. And no honest man could blame him for stopping me.

In order to speak in the way I have indicated, I should require permission to choose my subject. My speech would then show all the qualities that I claim for it. First of all, I would want to talk about the people of my native Rannafast and of the way they lived when I was young. Then I would describe the characters I knew, the things they did and the things they said, their songs and their stories.

That would bring me to the folklore. The sons of Usna fleeing with Deirdre from the wrath of King Conor. We see them being lured back and betrayed on their arrival.

We see them defending the Red Branch against the king's hirelings the livelong night. We see them captured at dawn by a treacherous ruse and being put to death... Next comes Cú Chulainn, a living picture of grief and misery, as he walks with a heavy step towards Magh Gine, his son's head in the one hand and his war weapons in the other.

From there I go on to the Fianna. I tell how Macán Mór, King of Sorcha, came to Ireland with a huge army. The invading fleet was first sighted away on the rim of the ocean, no bigger than seagulls. Nearer they come, their white sails bulging before the wind. Nearer and nearer still. Down past Inver Colpa, straining sheet and tack. At last they reached Ben Edair and they land. The Fianna met them on the beaches foot to foot and hand to hand. All day long the battle rages. At last Macán Mór is killed in single combat by Goll Mac Moirne. The hill and the beaches are covered with dead bodies ... The sun sets. Darkness begins to fall on Ben Edair. And the growling of hungry wolves can be heard in the distance as pack after pack of them comes swarming across Moynalty.

Continuing my 'speech before the House', I tell how Oisin was lured away to the land of perpetual youth by Niamh of the Golden Hair. I leave him there with his beautiful bride and his happy kingdom. I tell how the Big Fool comes to the land of Lochlann and surprises the Fianna in their sleep. I tell how the mighty Goll dies on a sea-girt rock because of its taboo for him to take the advice of a woman.

I could say all that, and a hundred times as much. But I could not utter one sentence in Irish about the Common Market or Free Trade or Protection or nuclear tests or radioactivity or commercial treaties or Human Rights or the Principles of Democracy. Not for thirty seconds could

I speak in Irish about any of the things that occupy (and must occupy) the thoughts of legislators today all over the world.

And why? Because the Battle of Kinsale was lost and with it the possibility of the Irish language becoming the vernacular of this nation. The clan system fell that day. Its fall was long overdue for it had outlived its usefulness. But unfortunately for Irish the clan system was abolished not by the native chiefs, but by England; and an English-speaking administrative system was set up in its stead. Had Ireland won that day and had England withdrawn as a consequence, things would have been fundamentally different. A centralised form of government would have been set up by the native chieftains on the ruins of the outworn clan system. Irish would have been the language of the new state - not on account of a clause in its Constitution, but by the very necessity of the case. The language would grow and develop as all languages do - again, by the necessity of the case. But the new system began and grew in the English language. And that finished Irish as our vernacular for ever.

Two centuries afterwards, Ireland had a leader who was a fluent Irish speaker. I mean Daniel O'Connell. In his day the number of Irish speakers exceeded the whole number of inhabitants of the island today. Yet even with over four million speakers of Irish it was clear to O'Connell that Irish could never become the vernacular of the people.

O'Connell was one of the greatest advocates of all time. 'Think of his speech for John McGee, the greatest forensic achievement since before Demosthenes'. Now let us suppose that O'Connell had been called on to defend John McGee before an Irish-speaking judge and jury. He could not have made that speech: he could not have delivered one sentence of it. There are no words in Irish for the things the great tribune has to say. Therefore we see that it was then impossible to replace English by Irish. And we are trying to do it now with only a few thousand native speakers left in the country - with only the scattered remnants of a dying *Gaeltacht*.

I would like to see as many as possible take an interest in Irish and studying it for its own sake. It is a beautiful language, even what is left of it. The study of it is a fine, intellectual exercise, and it often sheds a light on our past that no other language can. But even with this attitude of mind towards Irish, it would be sheer fantasy at this hour of the day to try to effect the replacement. To try to effect it by compulsion is positively criminal.

How long more are the people going to stand for it?

Yours etc.,
Séamus Mac Grianna,
275 Griffith Avenue Dublin 9.

COMPULSORY IRISH[4]

Sir,

When I entered into this controversy some weeks ago I knew I was going to bring heaps of abuse down on top of my head. Abuse is always the weapon of the man who has no reasonable argument to put up against the truth. He gets angry because he feels powerless. And the more vituperative he becomes the angrier he gets.

So I have an inferiority complex, I am a slave, a bogtrotter, a shoneen, a West Briton, a traitor, an ignoramus; and the latest indictment is for the atrocious crime of being an old man. If their vituperative vocabulary is running short I can give them more useful information. I am a bald-headed, short-sighted asthmatic. And then about my ancestors: I am descended from tinkers and thimble-riggers and so on, back to Éamann Bradach Mac Grianna, who was hanged for highway robbery about three centuries ago. This should be enough to have me treated as a hostile witness in any court of enquiry into the cause of our dear old tongue.

I am asked why I do not try to learn the new 'Irish'. I might if it were not for a deep impression that was made on my mind over forty years ago. I was one of a small circle whose object was to fight against what was known as 'Civil Service Irish'. There were six of us in the group, all native speakers, and we wanted a seventh. There is something magic in the number seven. At last we found him; he had spent only a few weeks in the *Gaeltacht* in his whole life. Yet we were unanimous in selecting him, which was a tribute to his ability and to his mastery of the language. I will call him 'X' for if he is alive, I am sure he has no wish to be drawn into a squabble about a cause that he has, perhaps, given up in despair long ago.

'X' was an inspiration to us all, and we spent many happy evenings planning how to advance our cause. We had many a good laugh. I remember one evening someone quoting the following relevant quotation from Fr. John O'Reilly's[5] book: 'Make up your minds in time to this: prigs and fools have not made languages. No, no, it has taken the eagles of the ages; and never doubt about it, it will take them again'.

And then from another came the comment: 'The men who are making the Civil Service Irish are anything but eagles. If I think of birds at all they put me in mind of moulting hens with bare red rumps scraping for worms on a dunghill'. That comment stuck in my mind and has influenced my attitude ever since.

Our little circle was called 'The Rollyers' (origin and growth of the word would take up too much space), and 'X' was one of our most brilliant members. I often ask myself if he is still alive. If he is, where is he? Has he given up all hope for the language? Is he sad and lonely? If he is, I am sorry, for

0, he had a grand Byronian soul
Forty golden years ago.

After this noble tradition and example the compulsionists want me to learn the new jargon. Some of them are in fact willing to give me lessons in it, beginning with easy steps - a word a day. The first word I am to learn is *minicíocht*. But I am afraid that I would get lockjaw if I tried to pronounce it. Then again I believe it was built on *minic*. And *minic* has far more meanings than are to be found in Dinneen. Take the following examples:

Is truagh nach tú an mhinic nach dtig
Is minic a chuaigh an mhinic chun fuaire.

And the one that would immortalise Jimmy Dhónaill if the *Gaeltacht* were not doomed to die:

Ba mhinic sin cnaipí ag ól bríste ar ghamhain.

One of my opponents says that 1916 has cancelled Kinsale. This surely calls for a drastic revision of the history of Ireland.

I am asked if I want to have the language back in the state it was under the British. Unhesitatingly I answer 'yes'. In my young days there was in Donegal an unbroken stretch of *Gaeltacht* over 40 miles long; and that was under the British. What do we find now after 40-odd years of native government? We find only patches here and there. And in the patches? Roofless homesteads, gaping walls, half-empty schoolrooms, seven schools closed, three or four more about to close, silent strands where children used to laugh and play in a bygone generation. This decay went on year after year while canting hypocrites continued to say at election that the language was the life and soul of the nation, and the *Gaeltacht* the life and soul of the language. But the lie became too obvious. The bubble expanded to bursting point. There was nothing for it but to make a new language that would be independent of the *Gaeltacht*. And that closes a chapter of our sad history.

I am asked why candidates who do their work 'through the medium' sometimes get higher marks in their examinations. Well 10% bonus marks is a nice little 'tilly' thrown in. But why do the candidates get the questions in both languages? For the simple reason that they would in many cases, fail to understand the Irish version. I have seen quite a number of these papers having eight children that sat for both Inter. and Leaving Cert. Exams. Another point: very often there are questions in maths where no language is used, for instance an equation in algebra. All you have to do is write *freagra* at the end instead of *answer*. Why not also write *réponse* or *antwort*? This would earn two more handfuls of marks, besides having the additional advantage of making us proficient in French and German, and so preparing us for the Common Market.

I am told it is a pity I am too old (my age again!) to study for a degree through the medium of Irish in University College, Galway. Now I happen to know quite a lot about university textbooks. I've never studied them but I've had to buy them in dozens. Where does U.C.G. get textbooks in Irish in Law, Medicine, Science,

Agriculture, Commerce etc? If they use English textbooks, they are not working 'through the medium'. Then what? Are we asked to believe that the students of U.C.G. are inspired, their school being the academic descendant of Clonard or Clonmacnoise?

A lady who replied to one of my letters said I would not admit that she knows any Irish. My fair opponent puts me in a very embarrassing position. She forces me to make the very unchivalrous disclosure that I know nothing about her Irish.

And finally the very friendly lady who said such things about my 'fine Irish' and warns me against joining the L.F.M.[6] I say to her: 'Too bad, darling: your warning was too late. I had joined the L.F.M. before your letter appeared'.

Yours, etc.
Séamus Mac Grianna,
275 Griffith Avenue, Dublin 9.
Language Freedom Movement.

COMPULSORY IRISH[7]

Sir,

In a previous letter I referred to the claim made for the success of some candidates who do their work through the medium of Irish, I could have added that on three occasions I have been asked by secondary teachers where they could get lists of terms to be used by their students at their exams. Each of them had the same story to tell. They were teaching through the medium of English, and set their pupils to memorise the terms a month or so before the exam. They made no secret of it. There was the ten per cent bonus marks, and, they had to compete with other schools!

It is sheer lunacy to think that any efficient teaching can be done except through the language of the person being taught. The first day a child goes to school, the good teacher will (if allowed) take the ideas and language in its mind and make that a starting point in imparting fresh knowledge. Going from the known to the unknown is the very foundation of teaching. Teaching the unknown in terms of the unknown is pure madness.

I think the controversy is getting too bitter, and bitterness never settled anything. Perhaps it would instill a little drop of Christian charity into our hearts and souls if we were to do a little bit of spiritual reading from time to time. I suggest that we begin with the *Acts of the Apostles*.

'If I come to you speaking in strange languages', says St. Paul, 'how shall I profit you? ... Even so ye ... unless ye utter with the tongue words of clear meaning how shall what ye say be taken in? You will be talking to the winds ... If I know not the meaning of the speech I shall be a barbarian to him that speaketh and he shall be a barbarian in regard to me. I speak in strange languages more than you all. Nevertheless in church I had rather speak five words with my understanding, so as to instruct others than ten thousand words in a strange language'.

Will those who advocate teaching through the medium of Irish outside the *Gaeltacht* tell us that St. Paul's teaching would have been more efficient if he had addressed himself in a strange language to the Corinthians, Romans, Galatians, Hebrews, etc., and offered them ten per cent bonus marks for understanding him?

But let us continue our spiritual reading. This time we go back to the Pentecost. 'Now there were staying in Jerusalem devout Jews from every country under heaven. And when this sound befell the multitude came together and was confounded, because each one heard them speaking his own language. And they were beside themselves with wonder, saying, "Lo, are not all these who speak Galileans? How is it that we hear each our own language in which we were born?"'

It should not be necessary to quote Pentecost and St. Paul, or even lesser authorities such as educationists or teachers, to prove that you cannot impart knowledge to any person except in a language that person understands.

It should be as plain as the noon-day sun to anyone with a pick of commonsense. If I want to learn to drive a car I must understand the language used by my instructor. If I don't I will get my skull cracked at the first hairpin bend I try to negotiate.

Recently a friend asked me why, now that my family are grown up, I should worry about our educational system. But I have grandchildren and it is only natural that I should feel concern for their future. Two of these grandchildren are in Dublin - Deirdre Nic Grianna and Helen Merry. It was on their account I entered into this controversy. One day as I sat watching them as they cooed and babbled in their cradles I asked myself what their destiny might be. Would Deirdre ruin another Ulaidh or Helen 'fire another Troy'? But all of a sudden the poetic vision vanished and I was face to face with stark reality .

I visualised them in four or five years being ruthlessly dragged into the Murder Machine. It was then I decided to add my feeble voice to the protest that was being made by the brave men and women who have faced the wrath and fury of the compulsionists.

This sets me thinking of my grandchildren in America. In my mind's eye I see a little girl of five years going to school in New York, and I imagine she can hear me when I say: 'Derval darling, they may say what they like about your native land. They may say it is full of crooks and gangsters. But there is no gangster to compel you to learn your arithmetic, etc., through the medium of the language of the Red Indians. No gangster to argue that it is the ancestral language of your country, and that America will never be a nation until she makes it her vernacular'.

Yours etc.,
Séamus Mac Grianna,
275 Griffith Avenue, Dublin 9.

Notes

1   *The Irish Times*, 19.5.66, 11. The following note is appended to the end of the letter: [Séamus Mac Grianna is the well-known novelist and short-story writer from the Rosses. 'Máire'. He has written many books, most of them in the nineteen-twenties and thirties, of which *Saol Corrach, Cith is Dealán*, and *Mo Dhá Róisín* are among the best known.] This letter started a heated debate in the *Irish Times* and participants in the ensuing correspondence included: B.S. de Róiste (24.5.66, 7), R.W. Johnson, Roisin Meehan (25.5.66, 9), Patricia Moore, Colm Mac Pháidín (26.5.66, 9) and Tomás Ó Céilleachair (2.6.66, 7). Some agreed with the sentiments expressed by Séamus but most of them disagreed strongly with them.
2   *The Irish Times*, 31.5.66, 9. The following responded to Máire: Charlotte G. Brooks (3.6.66,9), Anraí Mac Giolla Chomhghaill (4.6.66, 13) and Mrs. M. Fenton (16.6.66, 9).

3   *The Irish Times*, 10.6.66, 6. The following responded to Máire: Donn S. Piatt and Lil Nic Dhonncha (15.6.66,9), Micheál Ó hUanacháin (17.6.66, 4).

4   *The Irish Times*, 21.6.66, 12.

5   Fr. John Miles O'Reilly, author of *The Native Speaker Examined Home: Two Stalking Fallacies Anatomized* (Sealy, Bryers & Walker, 1909) is the person mentioned here and his views were often endorsed and quoted by Máire.

6   The Language Freedom movement was founded in 1966 and its aim was basically to put an end to what its members considered the over-advantageous status of the Irish language within the Republic of Ireland. Compulsory Irish within the education system was one of their main targets. What bound the members of the LFM together was '... *their concern for Ireland's future and the damage being done to it by an obsessed minority whose view was that Gaelic should and could become the Irish vernacular'* (*Gaelic Weekly*, 27.8.66, 1). The LFM published a list of their patrons in August 1966: *Professor George A. Duncan, M.A., LL.B. (Dublin), Alexis Fitzgerald (Dublin), Professor Michael G. Harrington, M.Sc., Ph.D. (Dublin), John J. Horgan, LL.D. (Cork), John B. Keane (Listowel), David Lane, FRCS, FRCSI (Dublin), Séamus Mac Grianna 'Máire' (Dublin), Denis J. Murphy (Cork), J.B. Roche (Newbridge), Senator Owen Sheehy Skeffington (Dublin), G.M. Wheeler., FCA, FCIS (Dublin)*. The Rev. Prof. (later Primate) Tomás Ó Fiaich called them '*English Irelanders*' (*Gaelic Weekly*, 16.7.66, 1). As against that, however, it was reported in the *Gaelic Weekly* (23.7.66, 8) that: '*The Sunday Independent called the entire Irish language movement a crowd of yahoos*'. As can be imagined, the LFM was a very controversial movement at the time but did not achieve its aims.

7   *The Irish Times*, 1.7.66, 9. N.M. responded on 5.7.66, 9.

Names

In traditional, Gaelic-speaking communities in Ireland, surnames were a rarity as so many families shared the same one. People were identified and particularised by placing after their Christian name that of their fathers or mothers e.g. John Chondy (Ir. Seán Chondaí lit. John son of Condy), Jimmy Elimy (Ir. *Séamas Fheilimí* lit. James son of Felimy), Bidí Vickey (Ir. *Bríd Mhicí* lit. Bridget daughter of Mickey) etc. Sometimes people were particularised by placing an adjective after their Christian names to denote particular features e.g. colour of hair John Roe (Ir. *rua* lit. red of hair), Mary Wawn (Ir. *bán* lit. fair hair), height John More (Ir. *mór* lit. big), place of residence etc.

Most of the names in these stories have been Anglicised, but some have been retained.

Place-names

All the place-names mentioned in these stories have been Anglicised.

GLOSSARY

achree	dear (Ir. *a chroí*)
aguisín	addendum
bán	white, fair-haired
binn	melodious, sweet
blasta	correct, well-spoken, tasty
brocach	freckled, pock-marked (Ir. *brocach*)
buí	blonde
cábánach	stay-at-home, unmanly person
cabar	eaves-knot (in thatching)
clout	a blow
crann smola	curse, blight
Cúirt na hÉigse	the court of poetry
feasach	knowledgeable
feis	Irish language and cultural festival
Gaeltacht	a rural community where the Irish language is the predominant language of communication
garbh	rough
geas	a taboo
keen	lament over a corpse (Ir. *caoin*)
leasrún	amendment
lúircíneach	weak, undersized person
masha	indeed, well! (Ir. *muise*)
ochone	exclamation expressing sorrow, vb. lament
poteen	illegally distilled whiskey (Ir. *poitín*)

Roe/ruadh	red (of hair) (Ir. *rua*)
scraw	a sod, scraw (Ir. *scraith*)
seanchaí	a story-teller
shoneen	flunkey, toady (Ir. *Seoinín*)
smugachán	contemptible person
soogan	spineless person (Ir. *súgán*)
teanga	language

Reader's Notes

Reader's Notes